Mackinac Heritage

Secrets of Mackinac Island

BK 6

Katie Winters

Chapter One

The pregnancy hadn't been an easy one. The normal stuff— morning sickness, heartburn, and food aversions hadn't been fun, of course. But beyond that, there was the fact that Emma had decided to have Grant Baxter's baby without telling him about the baby at all. Questions about the next phase of her life made her dizzy. Was she making a mistake? Would her baby resent her? Did she really have what it took to be a single mother?

According to her mother, Tracey Swartz, they didn't need Grant in the slightest. This wasn't such a surprise to hear. After all, Tracey had raised Emma basically on her own, with the help of her sister, Cindy, and her mother, Mandy. Men were nice to have around, especially if they were kind and loyal to you. But according to Tracey, they weren't necessary, not the way a mother's love was.

Emma had to take her mother's word for it.

After the terrifying flight with her father in August— which had nearly killed the baby— Emma had moved back into her childhood home with her mother. The story of Joey,

Emma's real father, was a doozy in and of itself. Because of him, Emma understood why her mother didn't believe Emma needed a man around at all. After only a day together, Joey had reminded Emma of Grant. It seemed she and her mother were both drawn to monstrous men.

Emma had worked at the fudge shop until it had closed for the season and now helped her mother with online orders from her downtown clothing boutique. Together, the two raked in a stellar revenue. This was especially lucky, as Mackinac Island had a very slow trickle of tourists once the winter season hit. Secretly, Emma adored the quieter season on the island. Most nights, she and her mother were cooped up in the cozy warmth of the house, watching television shows and movies or getting the nursery ready for the baby. They'd decided not to learn the sex, which had excited everyone in the Swartz family. Everyone had taken a bet. When asked which she preferred, Emma always said she didn't care— that ten fingers and ten toes on a healthy, little baby would do. Truthfully, she really wanted a girl.

It was now January. Emma's due date was only a few weeks away, which was terrifying. Although pregnancy had been a monster of a time in its own right, the reality of a baby would probably kick her in the face. How many diapers had she actually changed in her life? *What if the "mothering" instinct didn't kick in right away?* What if she was just a bad mom from the get-go?

"You about ready to go?" Tracey stepped into the kitchen and zipped up her winter coat, eyeing Emma where she sat at the kitchen table with a mug of tea. Outside, snow whirled past the windows.

"It looks chilly out there!" Emma smiled at her mother and tugged her hat over her ears.

Tracey grimaced. "I'll have Elise start the kettle now and have tea ready for us when we get there."

Now that Emma was nine months pregnant, it was a real spectacle to stand up. She went belly-first and quivered on legs that couldn't quite keep up with her weight. Once upon a time, she'd been a young and skinny twenty-something with nothing to lose. Everything had changed.

Outside, Emma and Tracey got on Tracey's snowmobile and adjusted their helmets over their heads. As there were no vehicles on Mackinac Island and Emma was as big as a whale, this was their main mode of transportation. It was very safe, mostly because Tracey went about five miles an hour and stopped at every stop sign for a good minute before going on.

It was six in the evening, and already, the sun had set. As they drove down the main road, warm orange light filled the windows, and the snowflakes glittered. The Pink Pony was hopping, as usual, and Marcy, the bartender and owner, could be seen near the back, hand on her hip as she took an order. Emma held her mother's arms tighter, and Tracey called back, "You okay? Should I slow down?"

Emma giggled. "No way. We'll never get there if you go any slower."

Elise and her new husband, Wayne, had recently purchased a very old and beautiful house up near the Pontiac Trail Head. Now, nearly everyone in the Swartz family lived along that road, save for Tracey, Emma, Uncle Alex, and Megan, who was away at Michigan State University. Grandpa Dean had joked they should rename the road "Swartz Road."

Since Elise and Wayne had purchased the old place, they'd thrown themselves into the redesign. Brad, Elise's son who normally lived in Los Angeles, had helped with construction, hiding away from whatever stress LA had given him. Emma had heard through the grapevine that his heart had been broken.

Now, Emma and Tracey stood on the front porch. Emma knocked on the door, listening to the roar of nourishing conversation on the inside. A moment later, Elise cracked open the door and called back, "Look who's here!"

Elise stepped back, smiling beautifully at both Emma and Tracey. As the door opened wider, all of the Swartz family came into view— leaping from behind the couch and the dining room table to call out, "Surprise!"

Emma's jaw dropped. Suddenly, she understood what this night was all about. This, the very first "family party" that Elise had decided to throw in her new house, was actually Emma's baby shower. Emma stepped through the door with tears in her eyes, making eye contact with each of the present family members.

"This is beautiful!" Emma opened her arms to her Aunt Else, who struggled to hug her because of her enormous stomach. Emma laughed. "It isn't so easy to get around these days."

"No problem at all! I remember those days," Aunt Elise said, gesturing toward a big, cozy green chair. "This is the guest of honor's seat for the night. Anything and everything you want — we'll get it for you."

"Finally, the queen is getting the attention she's always wanted." Megan stepped out from behind a pillar, her smile enormous.

Emma shrieked with surprise. "Megan! What are you doing here?"

Megan laughed and hurried toward her, careful to hug her from the side. "I wouldn't miss your baby shower, silly." She guided Emma to the green chair and helped her sit slowly, smiling the entire time. "How has it gotten so much bigger than Christmas?"

"You're telling me," Emma quipped.

"But you're glowing," Megan affirmed. "Your skin looks like peaches and cream."

"Ha. I don't feel like peaches and cream. But thank you."

Emma blushed, genuinely surprised. "Gosh, it's good to see you. Sit with me!"

Megan grabbed her glass of wine and joined Emma, squeezing her hand. Very soon after, Aunt Cindy came with a glass of non-alcoholic white wine for Emma. "Megan's right! You look gorgeous, my dear."

Over the next several minutes, her family members approached to say hello— Grandpa Dean, followed by Uncle Wayne, Aunt Cindy's boyfriend, Ron, Brad, her cousin Michael, and Michael's fiancé, Margot. Their baby was fast asleep in the next room. Unfortunately, Uncle Alex was nowhere to be found, nor was Penny.

"Alex wrote about a half-hour ago," Aunt Cindy reported. "He's stuck at work, tying up a few loose ends. He'll be here soon."

"Oh, good. We can't have a family party without him," Emma said. This, of course, wasn't entirely true, as Uncle Alex seemed to make a point to miss out on family parties left and right. Uncle Alex had never settled down and had any children, and Emma had a hunch this made him feel obsolete. It shouldn't have been this way, but families, as Emma knew, were complicated. The Swartz family was even messier than most.

"Penny wanted to fly back," Elise said, settling across from Emma with a glass of wine. "But she had a few auditions this week and couldn't swing it. She sends her love."

"Our little movie star," Emma joked. "I hope she can come over to visit soon."

Elise's eyes glittered with a mix of sorrow and love. "It's a horrible thing to live so far away from your children. Brad being around the past few months has been a godsend."

Emma nodded and furrowed her brow. Although her baby hadn't yet made it out into the world, she'd already begun to understand the intensity of love that came with motherhood.

How was it possible that one day, her child might want to live somewhere else— somewhere other than Mackinac? How could Emma allow that?

"Another great-grandchild." Grandpa Dean sat kitty-corner from Emma and shook his head. His eyes beamed with kindness. "I don't know how I got so lucky."

"Who wants enchiladas?" Aunt Cindy reappeared from the kitchen. "Elise, your new kitchen is just wonderful. The layout really works."

"Isn't it something special? I used to pull my hair out in my old kitchen in California." Elise stood to follow Aunt Cindy into the kitchen to help with the last of dinner.

With Brad in conversation with Grandpa Dean across the way, Emma and Megan were allowed a brief moment to chat.

"How are you feeling?" Megan asked softly.

Emma wrinkled her nose. "Like a blob."

Megan giggled. "I can't imagine what this feels like. It's weird, isn't it? We went through every life event together up until now."

"Now, you're experiencing college, and I'm experiencing the painful miracle of life," Emma joked.

"Ha." Megan punched Emma's arm lightly.

"Tell me something about college," Emma urged her. "I want to know more about your life."

Megan grimaced. "I went on a date the other night. For over an hour, he told me all about the field of podiatry."

Emma's jaw dropped. "Podiatry? Like, feet?"

Megan nodded. "It's a hard world out there."

"What happened to that guy you had a crush on? The one in your apartment building?"

"He had to move back home to take care of his mother," Megan said.

"What a good guy!" Emma sighed.

"All the good ones get away," Megan said.

Suddenly, the baby began to smash the feet into Emma's belly. The sensation was so strange. "Look!" Emma pointed at the vibration in her sweater, where the baby kicked. "They're talking to us."

"Hi, little baby!" Megan leaned closer to whisper to her belly. "We're going to be the best of friends, aren't we?"

Emma's eyes filled with tears. She hoped, beyond anything, that Megan would find a way back to Mackinac Island so that she could be a proper aunt to her child. Emma couldn't envision her future any other way.

A few minutes later, the family gathered around the dining room table to eat enchiladas and pour more helpings of wine. On another table set up to the side sat a beautiful cake in honor of Emma's baby, along with a wide selection of beautifully wrapped presents. Before they dug into the meal, Grandpa Dean said grace, thanking the Lord for the blessings they'd been given and asking for guidance and peace in the weeks leading up to Emma's baby's birth.

"Our family is about to get a little bit bigger, Lord," Dean said. "I pray that you watch out for us. And another thing. Wherever Alex is, I hope he receives your blessings, too. Bring him here tonight to celebrate with us. Our family isn't complete until he's under our roof."

Chapter Two

The Willow Bed and Breakfast was one of the only BnBs that remained open on Mackinac Island during the winter season. Because so many hospitality workers had left the island for the season, Alex Swartz himself spent a lot of his time at the Willow front desk, greeting guests who'd come to the island for a bit of its "winter charm" and gazing out the window at the fluttering snow.

That afternoon, Alex had checked out the final two guests and set himself up in the office to finish some paperwork before heading to his niece's surprise baby shower. Truthfully, he worked slower than normal, as big family parties tended to make him feel very small. His love for his family was enormous yet complicated. Decades ago, his father had cheated on his mother with a woman named Allison Darby, which had resulted in the birth of Elise Darby, his "new" half-sister. Alex's love for his mother was a very powerful thing, and forgiveness for his father's extramarital affair had been difficult to come by. Alex wasn't sure he would ever get over it.

On top of that, his three sisters were happy with children of their own, while he'd been mostly on his own throughout his entire adult life. His mother's death had ripped him in two, shedding light on just how lonely he truly was. Going to a big family party reminded him of that all the more.

Still, Alex loved his niece, Emma, so much that he was willing to force himself to go to the baby shower. Her pregnancy had been a difficult one, and he prayed every night for her safety and health. The baby blanket he'd purchased was forest green and very thick, and he liked picturing Emma all cozied up with her baby and the blanket as the winter months drifted toward spring.

Just as Alex began to pack up to leave, however, the front door of the bed and breakfast burst open. A young child's cry swelled through the bed and breakfast. Alex double-checked the bed and breakfast schedule, which had no guests listed for the next four days. *Who could it be?*

Alex headed out into the foyer to find a woman in perhaps her mid-thirties, along with two children under the age of four. The youngest one, around eighteen months old, had a tomato-red face and a very loud cry. The older one, maybe three, had his hand on his little brother's shoulder as he watched his mother try to calm him.

"It's okay, buddy. Really." The woman sounded on the edge of her own sanity. Slowly she lifted the boy into her arms and closed her eyes. The boy let out another horrible wail.

"Hello? Welcome to the Willow?" Alex stepped past the front desk, anxious and unsure of what to do to help.

The woman's eyes opened with surprise. Her older son blinked at him curiously.

"Oh, goodness. I'm sorry. I didn't see you there." In her arms, her little boy continued to cry.

"It's okay. I see it's been a tough night." Alex took another step forward.

The woman's eyes were lined with red. Clearly, the chilly

weather and the sorrow of being alone with two children had gotten to her. "It really has been." She bobbed her knees. "Do you have any available rooms for the night?"

Alex wanted to laugh and point out just how empty the place was. Instead, he replied, "Of course. Two beds, or just one with a toddler bed?"

"One with a toddler bed would be perfect." The woman exhaled all the air from her lungs. "I think he's sick."

Alex froze, conscious of how serious it was when toddlers were ill. "Does he have a fever?"

"I think so." The woman leaned back to try to look her son in the eye. She pressed her hand over his forehead and nodded, tears filling her eyes. "Is there a doctor we could call on the island?"

"Of course." Alex hurried behind the counter to find Doctor Miller's number. He was the only doctor who stayed on the island full-time during the year, as he'd recently retired from his mainland practice and decided to make the full move here. Alex quickly called the doctor and explained the situation. Doctor Miller said he could be there in twenty minutes.

"Let's get you settled up in your room," Alex said after he hung up. After a brief moment of thought, he selected the antique key for room eleven, which was a bit larger than the other single-bed rooms, with a gorgeous balcony that over-looked the Straits of Mackinac. Normally in the summertime, that room was booked out for months at a time. Although the room was pricier than the others, he already knew he wouldn't charge this woman full price. This was a rare thing for Alex, who made a point of looking out for the family business's bottom dollar.

"This way," he said, gesturing for the stairs. He then bent slightly and offered his hand to the anxious three-year-old, who'd remained quiet since they'd entered.

"Thank you." The woman blinked back tears, then added, "I'm Lily, by the way."

"I'm Alex." He smiled at her.

One by one, Alex helped the little boy up the stairs, calling ahead to Lily to tell her they were going to room eleven. Once there, he slid the key into the lock and opened the door to the luxurious room. Lily gasped and eyed Alex.

"Is this going to make me go bankrupt?"

Alex shook his head. "No, not at all. I just want you and your sons to be comfortable tonight. If you wait here, I can head down the hall to grab the toddler bed."

"Thank you, I really appreciate it."

Alex hurried down the hallway, feeling light as air. It had been a long time since he'd felt so useful, so necessary. The toddler bed was just where they'd left it at the end of the summer, and he carried it back to the room with ease. There, he set it up, his ears ringing with the little one's cries.

"He's been cranky all day," Lily explained. "But I thought he was just tired. On the ferry ride over here, the crying began, and it hasn't really stopped."

"Poor little guy." Alex shook his head. "I have some coloring books downstairs if your other son is into them?" The older son looked listless and unsure of himself, and it was clear his mother couldn't give him her full attention now that his brother was so ill.

"That would be fantastic," Lily said. "Are you my guardian angel?"

As Alex hunted for the coloring books downstairs, his sister, Cindy, texted him to ask where he was. Alex texted back: "work emergency," and left it at that. Just as he headed back to the staircase, Doctor Miller arrived, his cheeks bright red from the cold.

"Evening!" Doctor Miller gave Alex a nod and a very small smile. "It's a chilly one out there."

Alex stepped around the desk with an armful of coloring books and crayons. "They're upstairs." After a pause, he added, "I can't thank you enough for coming so quickly."

Doctor Miller followed Alex up the staircase toward the high-pitched screaming of the boy. When they entered the room, Lily turned, her eyes widening with hope at Doctor Miller's arrival.

"Well, hello there." Doctor Miller was friendly but serious. "Let's lie him here on the bed. Make him good and comfortable."

Slowly and carefully, Lily laid her youngest across the comforter. As she hovered over the doctor and her boy, her face echoed with anxiety. Again, Alex thought of his poor mother, who'd slept at his bedside all those months as he'd battled childhood cancer.

"Why don't I take your oldest downstairs?" Alex said suddenly, surprising himself with how put-together he sounded.

Lily blinked up. "Are you sure?"

Alex squatted down beside her eldest and tilted the coloring books to show off the pages and pages of empty dinosaurs and lions, tigers, and bears, all awaiting a young boy's scribbles.

"My name is Alex," he told him "What's yours?"

"Kevin," the little boy replied. He then took the dinosaur coloring book and waved it up and down.

Lily mouthed, "Thank you!" as Alex guided Kevin toward the door. Meanwhile, Doctor Miller was busy tending to the toddler. He pressed a stethoscope over his little heart.

Downstairs, Kevin was quiet and dutiful about coloring. Alex was reminded of himself, of how quiet he so often was in his own life as he tended to his father's many properties while the rest of the world had children and got married.

Sometimes, Alex interrupted Kevin's flow to ask him questions like, *"What is your brother's name?"* or, *"Where are you from?"* Each time, Kevin stopped coloring, lifted annoyed eyes, and said, *"His name is Ralphie,"* or, *"We're from Detroit."* As he was so young, he had trouble pronouncing words. Ralphie sounded more like "Ra-phee," and Detroit was "De-twoit." Alex knew better than to ask Kevin why his mother had brought her two little kids to Mackinac Island during the dead of winter, seemingly alone. There hadn't been a ring on her finger. *Where was their father?*

With the doctor still upstairs, Alex eventually remembered to text Emma.

ALEX: Hello! I am so sorry to miss your party tonight. There's an emergency at the Willow. I hope I can make it up to you. Love from your favorite uncle.

Emma wrote back a few minutes later.

EMMA: Oh no! Emergency? We hope you're okay.

Alex wrote back he was fine and that the emergency involved a guest, but a doctor had already arrived to help. As he pressed send, Doctor Miller stepped down the staircase and into the foyer.

"How'd it go?" Alex asked.

Doctor Miller spoke under his breath so Kevin couldn't hear him. "It's just a very bad cold. I've prescribed some medicine, and the boy should be able to sleep soon."

Alex breathed a sigh of relief. "Thank you again for coming by."

"Give me a call if you need anything else," Doctor Miller said. "And make sure all your guests get some rest tonight."

After Doctor Miller disappeared into the chilly night, Alex remained downstairs with Kevin for a good twenty minutes. He sensed Lily needed space. When she did appear on the landing of the staircase, she was alone, with more light in her eyes than she'd had since she'd walked in.

"Mama!" Kevin leaped from his chair and rushed toward her.

"Hello, my darling." Lily dropped down and lifted her other son to her hip. "You want to show me what you made?"

Alex stood expectantly. "He's asleep?"

Lily nodded and puffed out her cheeks. "His fever broke a little, and he's fast asleep for now. I can't thank you enough for calling the doctor. What a kind man."

Alex listened as Kevin showed off his collection of dinosaur pages. To each, Lily asked questions in a way that made it clear what kind of mother she was. She genuinely cared what her children told her.

"I'm going to take him upstairs," Lily explained after show-and-tell was over. "It's been a long day for all of us."

"Of course." Alex smiled and added, "If you'd like a nightcap after you get him to sleep, let me know. I'll be here all night."

Lily blushed, and a rush of fear came over Alex. Had he overstepped? Had he asked her to have a drink with him because he wanted to console her or because he was interested in her? It had been so long since he'd been interested in anyone; he couldn't tell the difference.

"That's so kind of you," Lily stuttered. "But I'm really too tired to be much of a conversationalist. Can I have a rain check?"

Alex smiled, knowing she didn't mean the "rain check" but grateful she pretended, anyway. "Of course. I'll have a break-fast spread out in the morning for all of you. Any special requests?"

"Nothing special. We're pretty easy. Cereal. Eggs. Anything." Lily gathered Kevin's coloring books and took Kevin's hand in hers. "Let's go upstairs, bud. Let's get some sleep." She then lifted her eyes to Alex's as she added, "Thank you again for everything, Alex. Have a good night."

"You too. As good as can be expected," Alex offered, watching as they ascended the staircase. When they disappeared, he sat in the empty foyer for a good five minutes, staring into space. Why did he suddenly feel so empty? Was it because, for a brief moment in time, he'd felt so necessary, so needed? Again, he questioned every decision he'd made in his entire life— and wondered if he'd missed his chance at happiness for good.

Chapter Three

The Monday after the baby shower, Emma and Tracey finished off the online orders for Tracey's Boutique at the kitchen table, packaging beautiful sweaters, luxurious cashmere scarves, and knee-high boots for women across Michigan, Illinois, Minnesota, Indiana, and Wisconsin. Emma propped some of the garments over her stomach as she worked, choosing to see her pregnant belly as a tool rather than a hindrance. Tracey chuckled and snapped a photograph as Emma said, "Stop that!" "You'll want a record of this someday," Tracey said. "Trust me."

Once the pile of packages was mountainous, there was a surprise knock at the door.

"Who could that be?" Tracey jumped up from her chair.

"You make standing up look so easy," Emma groaned and sipped her tea.

"Only a week or two left, baby girl," Tracey said. "Trust me. That child of yours won't let you sit down for long after that."

Tracey answered the door, crying out, "Look who the cat

dragged in!" Afterward came the stiff sound of boots on the welcome mat, followed by the sound of Uncle Alex's voice.

"I brought my present over," Alex explained. "I hoped I could give it to the new mother herself."

"She's right in here."

Emma prepared a welcoming smile for her uncle, who had skipped out on her baby shower for a "work emergency." He appeared in the kitchen with a brightly wrapped package and a smile of apology.

"Emma! Look at you!"

Emma waved her hand. "It's ridiculous. I know. I look like a beach ball."

Alex laughed and set the package on the kitchen table. He patted her nervously on the shoulder, clearly unsure of how to hug her. "I'm really sorry I missed your party. It was a hectic night at the Willow. A woman came in with a very sick child. I had to call Doctor Miller and help with her other son."

"Wow! A woman traveling alone with children during the off-season?" Tracey arched her brow. "Is she optimistic or just crazy?"

Uncle Alex and Emma laughed good-naturedly. Tracey stepped around Alex to put the kettle on the stovetop for tea. Alex, always nervous around family, sat next to Emma and said, "I hope you like the present."

Emma tore the wrapping carefully, then opened the box to find a forest-green, beautifully knitted baby blanket. She lifted her eyes to Uncle Alex, hopeful she could translate just how much he meant to her. "Thank you, Uncle Alex. Really. This is absolutely stunning."

"Oh. It really is!" Tracey rubbed the knitting with her thumb and first finger. "Hand-crafted."

"I hired a woman in Cheboygan to make it," Alex explained.

Tracey and Emma caught one another's eye, impressed. Alex puffed out his chest, clearly pleased with himself.

"You've outdone yourself, Al," Tracey teased. "Thank you."

* * *

Later that afternoon, after Alex went back to check on the mystery woman at the Willow, Tracey loaded up a cart with the packages and wheeled them to the downtown post office. This left Emma at home alone. Slowly, she inched toward the baby's nursery, where she hung the folded baby blanket over the side of the crib. Her heart was in her throat. It was difficult to imagine that in a week or two, a real baby would live there. A real baby who just happened to be her baby. *Was any of it real?*

As there wasn't a hospital on the island, Emma and Tracey had made preparations to stay in Cheboygan starting that Thursday. From their beautiful hotel suite, they would watch television, eat delicious meals, and mentally prepare for labor and delivery. When Emma's water broke, she would head to the nearby hospital, go through the most excruciating pain of her life, and ultimately return to the island with a baby.

Emma sat in the rocking chair in the nursery, which had been a gift from Elise and Wayne. There, she took in the decorations— the painting of the elephants along the river, the framed photograph of their entire family at Elise and Wayne's wedding, and the photo of Tracey with a baby Emma in her arms. Would this room belong to her baby for their entire childhood? Or would Emma eventually get a real job and save up enough to have her own place? *What would come next?*

A few minutes later came the sound of the front door. Tracey called out, "Where are you? You should have seen the line at the post office. Absolutely insane! I thought snail mail was dead."

Emma laughed and shifted forward in the rocking chair to prepare to stand. But as she pushed herself up, a terrible pain rocketed across her stomach, then along the bottom of her spine. As the pain mounted, fear overtook her. She collapsed back on the rocking chair and cried out. The sound of her own scream was animal-like. She hardly recognized it.

"Emma?" Tracey appeared in the doorway, stricken.

"Mom! Mom!" Emma gasped for breath. The pain seemed insurmountable. *Was this what it would be like to give birth?* "There's something wrong."

Tracey scrambled for her phone. Through the haze of her pain, Emma could hear her mother speaking to someone. Emma closed her eyes as another wave of pain enveloped her. She wanted to be unconscious. She wanted to be younger, a teenager, maybe, with her entire life in front of her. How had she ended up like this?

Minutes later, Emma blinked through another wave of pain to discover she was on her back in her baby's nursery. Doctor Miller, the island doctor, hovered over her. His fuzzy eyebrows were like caterpillars over his worried eyes. He spoke to Tracey as though Emma wasn't there. In some ways, Emma no longer felt like she was.

"My baby," Emma mumbled.

"It's okay, honey." Tracey's voice was low and soothing, however, it still had a slight touch of panic to it. Emma had only heard that voice a few times in her life.

"We're going to get you to bed," Doctor Miller told her. "There's not a whole lot I can do at this time. I'm calling a prenatal nurse I know on the mainland to come over this afternoon to examine you and the baby. How is your pain?"

Emma nodded slowly. "It's still there, but it's less."

"That's good." Doctor Miller sounded like he knew what he was talking about, but Emma wasn't so sure. Hadn't he just been a family doctor on the mainland before his retirement?

A few minutes later came the sound of more familiar voices. Emma recognized Uncle Alex's, then Uncle Wayne's. After that came Michael's. Apparently, someone had brought a stretcher from a nearby hotel swimming pool, and they planned to carry her on it from the nursery to her bedroom.

"This is so embarrassing," Emma said under her breath. Only her mother could hear.

"It's not," Tracey said. "These people love you more than anyone in the world. We're here to help you."

Very tenderly, Wayne and Alex shifted Emma onto the stretcher. Afterward, they lifted the stretcher and carried her to the bed, where they positioned the stretcher on one side and slowly eased her off. Emma had to admit: her mattress was a whole lot more comfortable than the nursery floor.

Despite this comfort, however, she was still panicked.

Tracey shooed everyone else out of the room. Uncle Alex, Wayne, and Michael sent her their love, and Doctor Miller assured her he would stay at the house until the nurse from the mainland arrived.

Finally, it was just Tracey and Emma in Emma's bedroom. Tears drifted down Emma's cheeks.

"What is happening, Mom?" She sniffed.

Tracey squeezed her hand. "We're going to get to the bottom of this. Try to breathe, okay?" Still, her eyes echoed with worry.

For the better part of an hour, Emma rose and fell from consciousness. Sleep was a blessing, as it allowed her to forget about the pain in her stomach and her fear of the future. Eventually, an unfamiliar voice came from the air above the bed, a woman who coaxed Emma back awake.

"Hello, hon. I'm Fanny." The woman was Doctor Miller's

friend, a prenatal nurse from the mainland. She'd brought tools to check on the baby, including a portable ultrasound machine. Emma was suddenly terrified of the machine and what it could tell her. It had the power to destroy her future.

After Emma was situated, with the cold goop across her stomach, Emma watched Fanny's face as she looked at the ultrasound on her screen. Her brow was furrowed, but her expression was difficult to read. She then checked Emma from the inside and the outside, snapped her gloves from her hands, and sat in a chair beside the bed.

"You're so close to giving birth," Fanny said, her smile slightly assuring.

"So close," Emma confirmed. "We planned to go to Cheboygan to wait for labor in just a few days."

Fanny shook her head. "I don't think you'll be getting out of this bed any time soon, I'm afraid."

Emma's heart sank. "But is the baby okay?"

"Yes. Your baby is fine." Fanny hesitated. "Your cervix is, unfortunately, on the thin side, which will make it very difficult for you to get around until your baby is fully ready for delivery."

Emma wasn't sure what to make of this. "A thin cervix?" It was strange to talk about her own body as though it was this other, separate thing.

Fanny nodded. "It's not unheard of. It can happen. I suppose the only problem is your given situation. You're not exactly close to a hospital."

"What about you?" Tracey asked from the other side of the bed. "Could we call you when she goes into labor? Could you come and help her give birth?"

"That is an option, of course. I often work at the hospital during the week, so it may be difficult for me to get over here."

Tracey and Emma eyed one another fearfully. *Had they*

waited too long to go to Cheboygan? Why hadn't another doctor caught the cervix issue?

"For now, you need to be right here in this bed as much as you can," Fanny continued as she began to collect her things. "I'll leave my number here, and you can call me whenever you need to."

Emma's tongue felt too thick; she struggled to speak properly.

"Over the next few days, I'll help you develop another plan," Fanny said. "For now, remember this isn't the end of the world in the slightest. Pregnant women go on bed rest all the time. Panic and stress only complicate things, so try to remain calm."

Emma snorted. *Calm? That was a tall order.*

Fanny nodded as she slipped her arms into her coat. "I know. It's not easy. But a month from now, when you hold your healthy baby in your arms, you won't remember this terrible time in the slightest. Keep your chin up. It'll be over soon."

Chapter Four

Alex felt helpless. He sat in the foyer of the Willow Bed and Breakfast with his hands in his lap and a forgotten cup of coffee in front of him, watching out the window as the water shifted across the winter beach. Only a few streets away, Emma was in the worst pain of her life. When Alex had been called to help move her from the nursery floor to her bed, he'd seen the fear written across her face. He'd understood the depths of her despair. Already, even before the baby was born, Emma was experiencing the true horrors of being a mother. A mother's life and happiness were completely tied up in her baby's. It had to be that way.

A family group chat without Emma's number had been started. Pings and vibrations came from Alex's phone. Elise had already begun to make a dish of lasagna to bring over. Cindy was on her way with other supplies. Wayne and Michael demanded answers as soon as the nurse arrived from the mainland. Everyone watched, expectant and fearful. *What would happen next?*

Suddenly, there was the stomping of very small feet,

followed by a friendly squeal. Alex turned to see Kevin whip across the foyer with a miniature airplane in his hand. He zoomed the airplane back and forth through the empty foyer, and his giggles echoed from wall to wall. Despite his fears for his niece, Alex couldn't help but smile.

Lily rushed down the staircase after him. Her brown hair whipped out behind her like a flag. "Alex, I'm so sorry! He got away from me as I was putting Ralphie to sleep."

Alex stood, watching as Lily wrapped her arms around Kevin and lifted her against him. "It's just fine. I was happy for the company." He smiled and was surprised it felt so natural.

Lily adjusted Kevin on her hip and stepped toward him. In the past few days, as far as Alex knew, Lily and her children had hardly left the Willow. As the Willow's normal chef was off the island for the winter, Alex had cooked very simple meals for them, making it his duty to research basic nutrition for children. Taking the food cart on the elevator, he'd wheeled up soups, chicken nuggets, steamed broccoli, and macaroni and cheese, along with more "adult" food for Lily, like burritos and salmon and chicken alfredo. Each time, Lily had thanked him profusely. Alex had to stop himself from thanking her back.

"How is Ralphie doing?" Alex asked now.

"His fever is almost all gone." Lily smiled wider. "He's acting more and more like his normal self."

"Such a relief."

"When my boys get sick like that, I lose my head. I hope I wasn't too much of a crazy person these past few days."

"Not at all."

Lily studied the foyer and the main sitting area, where Alex had built a small but cozy fire. "You don't happen to have any more coloring books, do you? Kevin is a miniature Picasso."

Alex hurried behind the front desk to produce two more coloring books, along with a fresh package of crayons. He then set Kevin up in front of the fire, watching as he selected a blue crayon and scribbled over a unicorn's stomach. When he turned back, he caught Lily watching him.

"I don't suppose I could have that rain-checked drink, now?"

Alex could hardly believe his ears. "What's your drink?"

"I'm a lightweight." Lily laughed. "A glass of wine sounds good. White."

"Coming right up."

Alex disappeared into the dining area to snag a bottle of chardonnay from the fridge, along with two glasses from the back. It was funny to walk through the restaurant during the winter season. The empty space seemed to echo the thousands of conversations that had taken place during the summer. Although Alex didn't think he believed in ghosts, when he'd seen *The Shining* for the first time, he'd understood the power hotels had. They carried secrets, affairs, and memories of life-altering decisions. They shimmered with life. And then, in the wintertime, where did all that energy go?

Back in the seating area, Lily rubbed her palms in front of the fire as Kevin colored on. A small part of Alex pretended Lily was his wife and Kevin, his son. This was just an everyday occurrence, a time to catch up after a long day.

"Here we are." Alex set both glasses on the coffee table and poured them stiff portions.

"Thank you." Lily lifted her glass and clinked it against Alex's. "You don't know what your generosity has meant to us."

Alex's eyes widened. He sat beside her, and the heat of her body beside his was overwhelming. He burned to ask her why she was on Mackinac. What had led her to this frigid rock in a lake in the middle of winter?

Instead, his phone buzzed several more times with texts from his family.

"That sounds like an emergency?" Lily eyed his pocket.

"My niece is pregnant," he explained. "Her due date is just a few weeks away. But today, something happened. The doctor put her on bed rest. Nobody in the family knows what to do." Alex's eyes filled with tears. "I'm sorry. I've just been sitting in this room, terrified for my niece. She's still so young. Twenty-four. A single mother. I keep wondering why there's so much pain in this world for those who don't deserve it."

Lily's lips parted with surprise. Alex, too, was shocked that he'd given her so much of himself so easily. He didn't open up to strangers, as a rule.

"Oh, Alex." She squeezed his elbow gently. "First of all, this young woman is very lucky to have an uncle like you. Someone who genuinely loves and cares for her."

Alex closed his eyes. He wasn't sure how lucky anyone was to have him in their life.

"Secondly..." Lily trailed off for a moment. "Pregnant women go on bedrest quite often. It's a precaution for many complications. Do you know anything else about her issue?"

Alex sniffed and read through his messages. Tracey had finally re-entered the chat with news of a thinning cervix.

Lily nodded. "Okay. That can happen." She brought her hands together, and her face was stoic. "Before my children were born, I worked as a midwife. I've delivered fifty-two babies. The number is precise; you never forget a birth, as they're all so different. Complications are a part of it all. I'm guessing your niece will need someone here on the island for delivery?"

Alex's jaw dropped. "You're a midwife? This time, you're my guardian angel."

Lily laughed softly, eyeing her son in front of the fire. "I would be happy to meet your niece and get a better sense of the situation. If your niece feels safe with me, I would then order the supplies necessary for the birth."

"You could have them delivered here. To the Willow."

"It's funny. I've felt more at home here at the Willow than I have just about anywhere in over a year." Lily laughed sadly.

Alex sipped his wine, unsure of what to say. "Do you and your children travel around often?"

"No. I've hardly ever taken them away from our home in Detroit."

Alex burned to ask her why. Then again, if she wanted to tell him, she would. He knew better than to probe into other people's business. Besides, she'd agreed to help Emma. What more could he want from her?

"Well, Mackinac is beautiful, no matter the season," Alex continued. "And there's something incredibly beautiful about being at the Willow without other guests."

"A bit spooky," Lily agreed. "But beautiful. Absolutely."

"Do you know how much longer you want to stay?" Alex asked.

Lily tilted her head thoughtfully. "Now that your niece is a part of the equation, I'm not sure. There's nothing calling us home very quickly. That's for sure."

Was she running from a husband? A lover? A family member? Was she using the Willow to hide? Alex was filled with questions.

Soon after, Alex found a way to liven up their conversation. They spoke of Ralphie and Kevin, about their likes and dislikes, and about Kevin's newfound confidence about being an older brother.

"I'm the youngest," Alex confessed. "Well, I thought I was the youngest. Turns out, my father had an extramarital affair. We just met Elise about a year and a half ago."

Lily's jaw dropped. There was an easiness between them, perhaps due to the wine. "That's so dramatic. Are you angry with your father?"

Alex sighed. "To be honest with you, my mother was my favorite person in the world. As a kid, I was very ill. Cancer.

She went everywhere with me to help me fight it. Miraculously, I survived."

"I take it you aren't exactly pleased your father betrayed her."

"No. Pleased is not the word I would use."

Alex and Lily locked eyes. Alex's heart pounded. It was clear he was attracted to her. Still, there was no way he could make a move. Was there?

"Well." Lily sipped the last of her wine. "I think it's about time I got Kevin to bed. Thank you for the wine and the conversation. Really. It's a rare thing that I speak to someone over the age of three."

"Any time."

Alex watched as Lily gathered her eldest and walked slowly to the staircase. Already, Kevin was slumped in her arms, fading into sleep.

Alex then dialed Tracey, overwhelmed with his desire to help. Tracey answered on the third ring.

"Alex. Hi. Thank you so much for your help today." She spoke too quickly.

"Don't worry about it. Hey, listen. Remember the woman who's staying at the Willow?"

"The one with the children?"

"Yes. Apparently, she's a midwife. She's delivered fifty-two babies. Can you believe it?"

Tracey was flabbergasted. "You're kidding."

"Should I bring her over tomorrow?"

"Please, Alex. Please do." Tracey sighed for a very long time. "From the bottom of my heart, thank you. All I can do right now is worry. Knowing there's somebody close by who could help is a Godsend."

Chapter Five

The next morning was grim and gray. Out of Emma's window, rain mixed with snow, and a naked tree shivered in the wind. This was Emma's only view of the outside world. This was the mundanity of bed rest. Worst of all, it was only the beginning.

Of course, with a mother like Tracey, things were always interesting. Very soon after Emma awoke, Tracey appeared in the doorway with a platter of pancakes, scrambled eggs, strawberries, blueberries, and turkey bacon, chatting excitedly about the day ahead. Emma positioned herself slightly on her side with the breakfast tray next to her, and she stabbed a strawberry with her fork as her mother said the words "midwife" and "Alex."

"Excuse me? What did you say?" Emma turned as the strawberry's flavor exploded across her tongue.

"Alex has a midwife staying at the Willow." Tracey sat cross-legged on the bed like a teenager. "He's bringing her here today to check on you and talk about the process. She's delivered fifty-two babies!"

Emma was surprised. Not only that, but a feeling of calm also took over her, one that made her realize just how panicked she'd been since the day before. Even her dreams had been nightmares.

"Aren't you relieved, honey?" Tracey squeezed Emma's knee over the comforter. "This is your first day of bed rest. But I have a hunch you won't be here long, and we'll have that little baby out here in the real world in no time. Someone is watching out for us."

About two hours later, after Emma had eaten breakfast and watched two episodes of a very cheesy dating show, the doorbell rang. From bed, Emma could hear Tracey greeting Uncle Alex, along with the midwife. Children scrambled and squeaked in the living room. Although they were loud, the sound was reassuring. It was a reminder that healthy babies were born all the time.

Tracey opened the door a moment later and led the midwife into Emma's room. The midwife, who introduced herself as Lily, was in her mid-thirties, with a beautiful and comforting smile. Emma could understand why she'd been such a prosperous midwife. You looked at her, and you felt safe.

"How are you feeling, Emma?" Lily asked as she sat on the chair beside the bed. "I understand your cervix is quite thin."

"That's what they tell me."

"It's not uncommon. It's just important we monitor the situation going forward. I've delivered more than my share of babies at home. Normally, I build relationships with the mothers months ahead of time to ensure an easy home birth. This time, we have only a few weeks. We'll have to make do."

"You don't know how happy I am you're here." Emma's voice caught in her throat. "Yesterday was terrifying."

Lily nodded. "I can understand that. There's nothing worse than thinking your baby's health is at stake."

"And you're willing to stay on the island a little while longer?" Emma asked. "I know you're just a guest at the Willow. I hope this won't keep you from anything at home."

A strange look passed over Lily's face, one she immediately corrected with a smile. "My main focus right now is you and your baby's health. My sons and I came to Mackinac without a real plan. We're happy to stay for as long as it takes."

Although this again reassured Emma, it did pique her curiosity. *What sort of mother could just whisk her children off to Mackinac Island in the middle of winter like that?*

"Your sons sound adorable," Emma said instead of asking the questions she really wanted to ask.

"Alex has really taken to them." Lily swept a curl behind her ear. "It's been a little while since they had a man around. I think they're fascinated with him."

Emma dropped her gaze for a moment. *Did this mean the woman's husband had died?*

Before she could speak, Tracey saved the conversation. "Alex has always adored kids. He was always playing games and running around with Emma and her cousins."

Lily's cheeks were bright pink. "When we first arrived, my son had a terrible fever. I was at my wits' end, to tell you the truth. Alex flew in like Superman and saved the day. I've been able to rest easier, just knowing he's watching over us at the bed and breakfast."

Emma and Tracey exchanged glances just for a split second. It was clear this woman had a blooming crush on Uncle Alex. Emma had never known her uncle to have a girl-friend, not even in the summertime when passing flings were popular.

Over the next forty-five minutes, Lily performed all the rituals of a midwife. She checked the baby's heartbeat, examined Emma herself, and then returned to the chair beside the bed to discuss the "birth strategy." Nothing about this had been

Emma's plan, but she found herself leaning into it, trusting Lily's every word.

After Emma had peppered Lily with questions that ranged from silly to serious, Emma heard herself say something much too personal.

"I'm terrified to bring a baby into the world without a father." She paused, furrowing her brow. Lily didn't look surprised. "I hope I'm not making a mistake?"

"I take it you haven't told him."

Emma nodded, her eyes filling with tears.

Lily touched Emma's hand. "So many women have been in your shoes on this one. But only you know what's right. If your instincts tell you not to share this with the father, then you have to listen to them."

A squeal from one of Lily's boys came from the living room. Emma laughed gently.

"They seem okay," Emma suggested.

Lily's eyes shifted. "Yes. Well." She shrugged. "Their father hasn't been around for a little more than a year. We've found our ways to adapt."

"What happened to him?" Emma was stricken, fearful of the numerous ways life could be destroyed.

"I actually don't know. I know that sounds ridiculous. But one day he was in our lives, and the next day, he wasn't. I suppose I shouldn't be surprised. People have been falling out of my life like water through my fingers. I just never imagined he'd go, too."

"Goodness." Tracey shook her head.

"I'm so sorry that happened to you," Emma whispered.

"I'm sorry, too." Lily tried to smile.

"I raised Emma without her father around," Tracey admitted. "I never told him about Emma at all until this year, actually. I ran into him at an airport in Los Angeles, of all places."

"After that, all hell broke loose," Emma joked.

Tracey flashed her a dark look. "It's true. I never should have tried to welcome him into our lives. He was never worthy of us, of what we've built here. He was never worthy of our love."

Lily stitched her eyebrows together.

"What I mean to say is, it's clear your children's father never understood what he had." Tracey straightened her back and looked Lily directly in the eye.

"That doesn't mean I don't miss him," Lily responded quietly.

"Missing people is a part of life. It's difficult, but I try to focus on how grateful I am for the people I have." Tracey blinked back tears. If Emma had to guess, Tracey thought now of Malcolm, the handsome film director out in Los Angeles she'd fallen in love with over the summer. The one who'd gotten away.

"It's a constant struggle," Lily agreed. Her smile widened as she took in the very pregnant Emma and her beautiful mother. "But conversations with women like you help me through."

Emma and Tracey bid goodbye to Lily, who retreated into the living room to gather her children. Before he left, Uncle Alex dipped his head into the bedroom to say hello. His cheeks were ruddy from playing, and there was a light in his eyes.

"How are you doing, Em?"

Emma waved a hand from behind her massive pregnant belly. "You know. Just another day as the most pregnant woman in the world."

Alex laughed. Then in a soft, quiet voice, he asked, "What did you think of Lily?"

"She's amazing," Tracey said. "Really. Thank you for bringing her here."

"Yes. I can't tell you how much better I feel." Emma smiled.

Alex breathed a sigh of relief. "Good. Great, actually. She

and her sons are the only guests at the Willow right now. Me and the boys have really taken to each other, and I was terrified she would leave soon."

"I'll keep her trapped here for a little while longer," Emma joked.

After Alex, Lily, and her sons disappeared into the chilly afternoon, Tracey and Emma propped themselves up on pillows, ate grilled cheese sandwiches, and watched trash television. Between episodes, they spoke of Lily, of the sorrow in her eyes when she spoke about the man who'd left her and her children behind.

"This is just what I keep telling you," Tracey said, her eyes widening. "A mother's love is always enough."

Emma nodded along, unsure if she fully believed her mother or if she just wanted to. Nevertheless, she felt enshrouded with love and entirely grateful. Very soon, Lily would help her bring her baby into the world— and after that, she would know the full dimensions of motherly love.

Chapter Six

The next morning, as usual, Alex wheeled the breakfast cart onto the Willow elevator, pressed floor two, and stood in silence as he was lifted to Lily, Kevin, and Ralphie. Breakfast was eggs, bacon, fruit, potatoes, orange juice, and coffee for the adults. Alex had even tried to make the pancakes into dinosaur shapes. They'd turned out like blobs.

Lily opened the door to reveal a chaotic yet endearing morning. Kevin bounced up and down on the bed while Ralphie blinked out from his toddler crib and squealed with joy at Alex's arrival. Lily was a mess. Her hair was uncombed, and she wore a massive t-shirt and baggy shorts. Alex had never seen anyone more beautiful in his life.

"Come in! Come in." Lily beckoned him and the food cart in, just as she always did. He set it up next to the little table along the window. Already, Kevin clambered into his typical seat and cried, "Breakfast!"

"He's been talking about you ever since he got up," Lily said with a gentle smile.

Alex blushed. "I've never been so popular before."

"You should stay for breakfast!" Lily suggested, which is what she did every morning. Alex always said yes. He'd cooked way too much food for just her and the kids, anyway.

Alex sat at the breakfast table with his fake family, pouring orange juice, slicing pancakes, and helping Ralphie eat his eggs. It was loud and funny and messy. Often, Alex ended up with eggs in his hair or orange juice on his button-down. He didn't care. He would have swum in orange juice if it meant impressing Lily and her children.

"How's your time on the island been so far?" Alex asked Lily between the children's screeches. He knew she and the kids had been out for a few walks over the past few days, seeing the sights and stopping at The Grind, Wayne's coffeeshop.

"Oh, it's just so beautiful here," Lily said with a sigh. "And I can't get over just how wonderful your sister and her daughter are. It had been a long time since I'd had such a nourishing conversation with another woman."

Alex was intrigued. Like him, did Lily not have many friends? He wanted to learn more about her. But before he could ask, Ralphie whipped his hand back and forth on the table and made his sippy cup clatter to the ground. Both Alex and Lily jumped for it and nearly smashed skulls. They laughed.

"You're too good to us," Lily said. Her smile was heaven.

"You're our honored guests here at the Willow," Alex reasoned. "It's my pleasure." He then swallowed some coffee, his stomach bubbling with fear. "I would love to show you around sometime. Maybe even without the kids if you'd be up for it."

Lily's lips parted with surprise. He'd asked her out— and she looked shocked. He'd overstepped. Why was he so stupid?

But instead of skirting around the issue and making an

excuse, she said, "That sounds wonderful. Oh, but I don't know of any babysitters around here."

Alex could hardly believe his ears. "My entire family lives on the island. I'm sure I can find someone to watch the kids for the night."

Lily's eyes brightened. "I can't remember the last time I had a break. Gosh, six months ago? Eight?"

"Let's make it happen."

* * *

Cindy answered Alex's call without saying hello. "Tracey says you have a new woman friend."

"Hello to you, too." Alex's smile widened. "Is it true you and Tracey are the biggest gossips on the entire island?"

"We've held the title forty years running," Cindy joked. "But seriously! Alex! Who is this woman? Tracey says she's a midwife. That she's going to deliver Emma's baby."

There in the Willow office, Alex puffed out his chest. It had been ages since his sisters had dug into his business like this. It felt ridiculously nice that they cared.

"Her name is Lily, and she's just a guest at the Willow," Alex said. "Luckily, she's a midwife, which makes Emma's situation a whole lot less worrisome." He paused, willing himself to be brave. "And tonight, I was wondering if you could find it within yourself to babysit her children, so I can take her out."

"A date!?" Cindy's shriek filled Alex's ear. He ripped the phone back, surprised he didn't hear Cindy's cries over the hills of Mackinac Island itself. The island wasn't so big.

"Calm down, sis." Alex rolled his eyes. "Lily has been through a lot. I'd just like to take her out for the night."

"I'm sorry. I'm sorry." Cindy laughed. "I just can't remember the last time you took a woman out."

Alex leaned against his desk, gazing out the window at the

fluttering snow. Truthfully, he was light as air and more hopeful than he'd been in years. Still, he wasn't sure he could allow himself to trust this. Not until it stuck.

"We were thinking of heading out around five for a walk, followed by dinner and a few drinks," Alex said.

"She has two boys?"

"Adorable boys."

"Oh, Alex. You're in love."

"I am not."

At four-forty-five that afternoon, Alex waited for Lily and the boys in the foyer. He wore a pair of jeans and a black button-down, and he'd gelled his hair slightly to give it "volume," as the internet said. When Lily and the boys appeared on the staircase landing, Alex's heart nearly exploded with fear. In a fuzzy white sweater, a pair of jeans, and light makeup, Lily was more beautiful than ever.

"It's so nice of your sister to babysit," Lily said, interrupting Alex's stunned silence.

Alex touched his hair. "She loves kids."

"That's a rare thing," Lily affirmed, dropping down to zip Ralphie's coat. Alex followed her lead and zipped Kevin's, feeling important.

Up at Cindy's, she welcomed the little boys with open arms. Ralphie and Kevin rushed into the warmth of her big, beautiful house, accepting her peace offering of hot cocoa and art projects. Lily shook Cindy's hand and thanked her for her help, again explaining that she hadn't had a night off from being a mother in "quite some time."

"It's necessary for your mental health," Cindy affirmed. "You have to take care of yourself first."

Lily kissed her boys goodbye, turned on a heel, and followed Alex from the house. Cindy waved and closed the door, leaving them in the chill of the front porch. Lily laughed and dropped her head back.

"I miss them already," she said. "And I'm only half-joking."

"I can only imagine what that's like," Alex said. He wanted more than anything to take her hand, but instead, they both tucked theirs in coat pockets and sauntered down the porch steps and onto the road.

From the Pontiac Trail Head, you could see the glittering Straits of Mackinac and the entire five-mile strip of the Mackinac Bridge. Alex had hardly gone a day without seeing that view in his life, which meant instead of looking at it, he looked at Lily's face as she took it in.

"It's stunning." Her breath became foggy. "Can you even really see it anymore? Or is it just background to you after an entire life on the island?"

Alex laughed, surprised that she'd read his mind. "I'm spoiled here on the island. I have to remind myself of that, over and over again."

Down they went from Pontiac Trail Head through the stoic and abandoned grounds of the Grand Hotel. Alex explained his half-sister's wedding had just taken place there in October and that many movies had been filmed there over the years. He didn't mention it had also been where his father had cheated on his mother with Allison Darby. As he loved the Grand Hotel, he didn't always want to associate it with such dark times for his family.

Afterward, Lily and Alex walked through downtown, chatting about the fudge shops, Tracey's boutique, and the chaos of the summertime, when each hotel and bed and breakfast was full, and horses tugged carriages along the cobblestone streets.

"It's like a fantasy," Lily said.

"I can't believe you never came up here. You're from Detroit, right? It's not so far."

"It's terrible, isn't it? I don't know what my parents were thinking."

"Where are your parents these days?"

Lily grimaced. "They're both gone, unfortunately. I lost them before my boys were born."

"Oh no." Alex stopped for a moment, annoyed at himself for being so flippant about something so serious.

"Don't worry about it." Lily touched his arm. "You couldn't have known."

When their walk became too chilly, they ducked into a pizza place on Main Street and ordered a pizza to share, along with mozzarella sticks and a salad. Lily suggested a Zinfandel wine, which Alex was impressed by. As they ate, they chatted easily about Ralphie and Kevin and about Alex's duties for the hotels and bed and breakfasts.

"My dad is mostly retired and lets me handle everything," Alex explained. "And I'm very proud of what we do. Working in hospitality is no easy feat. But every day, you find little ways to make someone's trip."

Lily's eyes sparkled from the light of the candles.

"Although I shouldn't be talking about making someone's trip. You're a midwife, for crying out loud. You bring people into the world. How did you get into that?"

Lily dabbed her perfect lips with her napkin. "Through my teenage years and my early twenties, I was really floundering. I worked at restaurants and bars and dated a string of bad guys. The only thing I knew for sure was that I liked to help people. One evening, after a particularly bad breakup with another loser, I met an old friend who was very pregnant. She went into labor while I was with her, and I rushed to the hospital to hold her hand. It was the most intoxicating and beautiful experience. When I saw her hold her baby for the first time, I had this sense that everything in life was worth it. Maybe that sounds silly."

"It doesn't." Alex was quiet yet firm. "You want your life to mean something. That's so rare. And beautiful."

Lily blushed and took a sip of wine. Alex felt as though

they lived out a romantic film, one that involved kisses in the rain and whispered words in bed. Would he ever be allowed such love?

After dinner, Lily and Alex walked to the Pink Pony, where Marcy and her boyfriend, Kurt, stood behind the counter. Love and flirtation buzzed between them. As Alex and Lily slid into a booth, he whispered, "Kurt has been waiting for Marcy to realize she's in love with him for decades. They finally got together a couple of months back."

"What a romantic story!" Lily breathed.

Before they could talk more, Marcy approached the booth with menus and a smile. Since her romance with Kurt had begun, she'd been vibrant and bubbly, teasing the bar patrons and getting in on island gossip. It was funny to see.

"Hi again!" Marcy greeted Lily and tapped her shoulder. "I didn't know you two knew each other."

Alex tilted his head. *How did Marcy know Lily?*

"My sons and I are staying at the Willow. Alex has been a gracious host," Lily explained.

"The Swartz Family certainly knows their way around a bed and breakfast. By the way, Lily, I've thought about you a lot the past few days. Have you had any luck?"

Alex's lips parted with surprise. *Luck with what? What was Marcy talking about?*

Lily blushed. "Unfortunately not." She then grabbed a menu, studying it like it was an important text. "I'll have a mojito, I guess. And Alex?"

"A beer," Alex said, locking eyes with Marcy.

As Marcy traipsed back toward the bar, Alex stumbled over his words. "So, you know Marcy?" But before she could answer, the bell on the door jangled. Two newcomers entered— the newlyweds, Wayne and Elise. Alex's heart sank.

"Hello, there!" Elise's grin was enormous. She was clearly

pleased to have run into Alex and his "mystery woman." As usual, Tracey and Cindy had filled Elise in on everything.

"Hi." Alex palmed his neck as they approached. "Lily, this is my half-sister, Elise. And this is her husband, Wayne."

"I think I saw you at the coffee shop," Lily said, shaking both of their hands. "It's a pleasure to meet you. I know Alex is related to about half the island, so it's not so strange to run into one of his sisters at the only open bar in town. Then again, I'm from Detroit, so any kind of coziness is strange to me. Would you like to sit down?"

Alex was split. On the one hand, he was so grateful to his family for opening their arms to Lily. On the other, he wanted Lily all to himself on their first date! Was that too much to ask?

Wayne clapped Alex on the shoulder. "We shouldn't interrupt them," he said to his new wife.

"Nonsense," Lily said. Under the table, she reached across and squeezed Alex's hand. A jolt of electricity went up and down Alex's spine. She liked him. She really liked him.

Marcy approached to take Elise and Wayne's orders, a glass of wine and beer, respectively. Afterward, Elise and Lily chatted easily about the island, Tracey's boutique, and Emma's pregnancy. This left Wayne and Alex alone.

Normally, Alex felt strange around Wayne. Wayne was a man's man, the sort of "hero" type who'd swept Elise off her feet after she'd come to the island. Alex was shy and very unsure of himself around women. He prayed Lily wouldn't compare the two of them and decided Alex came up short.

"Your sisters won't stop talking about this newcomer, Lily," Wayne said quietly, careful not to speak too loudly.

"Ha. I'm sure." Alex sipped his beer.

"She seems fantastic. So friendly." Wayne arched his brow. "And now that I have stepchildren of my own, I can only say they're a blessing. Brad and I hang out all the time these days. He's hilarious."

Alex tried to suppress a grin. "This is only our first date. Talking about stepchildren is usually reserved for dates two or three."

"What are you two talking about over there?" Elise lifted her chin.

"Alex was just telling me about the ins and outs of hospitality," Wayne boomed back. "Since you're a writer, you can't understand hard labor. I know that."

Elise stuck out her tongue playfully.

"You're a writer?" Lily asked, intrigued.

"Screenplays, mostly," Elise said.

"She's brilliant," Wayne offered.

"Her movie was just made into a film over the summer. Right here on Mackinac," Alex boasted, loving the way Lily's eyes danced as she spoke with all of them. He could already imagine her at a Swartz family party, chatting with everyone. His dad would adore her.

"And Tracey worked in the costuming department," Elise said.

"You're kidding. I can't wait to see it when it comes out!" Lily cried. "Who knew Mackinac Island had so many connections?"

"It's a magical place," Elise said, her eyebrows raised.

After a drink and then another, Lily and Alex admitted they had to "save" Cindy from the boys. Elise and Wayne were disappointed yet understanding. They hugged them both goodbye and waved them out until it was just Alex and Lily on the sidewalk outside the bar. In the silence, Alex felt at peace. It had been a remarkable night, one he would never forget. It was strange that "normal" people had nights like this all the time.

As they wandered back up to the Pontiac Trail Head, they eased from one conversation to the next. A heavy moon hovered in a dark blanket of stars. When they reached the beautiful road at the top of the hill, Alex got up the nerve to turn to Lily, touch her arm, and ask, "Can I kiss you?" To this, Lily tilted forward and planted her lips against his. For a moment, all Alex knew was the warmth of her body pressed against his and the soft pillow of her lips. For the first time in a very long time, he was so grateful he'd survived as a child. He could now experience life to the fullest.

When their kiss broke, they gazed into one another's eyes for a long time. Alex had no idea what to say.

"That was. Um. Wow." Lily smiled.

Alex nodded. "I like you, Lily. In case that wasn't obvious."

Lily nodded and closed her eyes. "I like you, too." Then, there was a pause. Alex's heart filled with dread. "The thing is, I don't know how long I'll be here on the island."

Alex's shoulders dropped. She had another life somewhere. That was clear.

"But I'm so glad I met you, Alex. You've been a bright light."

"I'm glad I met you, too."

Again, they gazed at one another, overwhelmed with feeling. Alex wanted to kiss her again so badly, but he was terrified she would push him away.

"We should get the boys," Lily said finally, lifting her thumb toward the big house.

"You're right. They're waiting."

Alex and Lily walked wordlessly toward Cindy's house, which was all lit up, its big windows aglow and a fire crackling in the fireplace. It was home in every sense of the word— much more than Alex's place, where he resided alone.

Chapter Seven

The days of bedrest were long, punctuated with breakfasts, lunches, dinners, snacks, and funny conversations with Tracey. Beyond anything, Emma was bored. Even the dating shows that had previously been distracting were boring now. Her belly even seemed to get bigger by the day, as though the baby planned to trap her in the bed forever.

Twice that week, the midwife, Lily, stopped by to check on Emma. Because she spent so much time worrying about the baby (because she had nothing but time), the health visits cleared Emma's mind a great deal. When Lily announced she'd ordered supplies for the birth, both Emma and Tracey squealed with excitement. The birth was a very real thing that would eventually happen. They had to be patient.

After six days of bed rest, Emma was propped up, trying to read a book, when she heard a knock at the front door. Tracey answered it and cried out, "Uh oh! We've got a visitor."

Emma froze. Excitement was a very rare thing in that house. Slowly, she placed the book to the side of the bed and watched the shadows in the hallway. Then, Megan appeared, rushing toward her with her backpack bouncing against her back.

"What are you doing here!" Emma cried as Megan scrambled onto her bed and gave her a hug and two kisses on the cheek.

"You think I can just hang around East Lansing while you're stuck in bed like this?" Megan demanded.

Emma grimaced. All week, she'd felt annoying when she'd texted Megan. She'd wanted news of the outside world, anything that distracted her from her bedrest life.

"You really didn't have to come," Emma tried to insist. "You have a life outside these four walls. You should be living it!"

"Don't be silly." Megan opened her backpack and showed off a package of donuts from an East Lansing donut shop, along with a bottle of alcohol-free wine. "Plus, I asked a few of my teachers if I could take online classes for the next week or two."

Emma's jaw dropped. "You shouldn't have done that!"

Megan shrugged and began to crank open the non-alcoholic wine. "It's not like I can't do everything online, anyway."

"What about your friends? What about dating?"

"You're more important," Megan said simply as she yanked the last of the cork from the bottle. "Why do they put corks in non-alcoholic bottles, anyway? Is it just for show?"

Emma laughed as Tracey appeared in the doorway. "Nothing can keep you two apart, can it?"

Emma's heart lifted. As Tracey disappeared to grab the glasses, she clutched Megan's shoulders and said, "You don't know how bored I've been!"

"I have a hunch," Megan said. "Every day of the past week, you've asked me what I had for lunch and dinner and what I wore to class. Those are warning signs."

Tracey returned with glasses for the girls and retreated, closing the door. Emma and Megan clinked wine glasses and giggled, feeling like schoolgirls. "It's like when we snuck wine into your room in high school," Megan breathed.

"How times have changed!"

Megan nodded. "Tell me what's been going on. Mom said something about a midwife. And about how Uncle Alex is falling for her?"

"It's been a whirlwind. Apparently, Uncle Alex and my midwife went out for pizza and drinks at the Pink Pony the other night."

"Uncle Alex? Falling for someone? I never thought I would see it. What's she like?"

"Lily is seriously smart. Some of the stuff she's told me about pregnancy and childbirth is brand-new information for me. She's delivered over fifty births!"

"Can you imagine having such an important job?" Megan breathed. "Oh, and what do you think she thinks of Alex?"

"Apparently, Aunt Elise hung out with them at the bar, and they seemed really happy!"

"I'm glad the island is still up to its ears in gossip," Megan said. "Mom said she babysat the kids. Apparently, they talked about Alex a lot. Can you imagine Alex as a stepdad?"

"He looks like a completely different person."

"They say that happens when you meet the one." Megan furrowed her brow and opened the package of donuts. "Did you feel that way when you met Grant last summer?"

"Oh, gosh. Grant." Emma closed her eyes, and all she could see was Grant's face. "He was so handsome. And so damaged. I never knew what he was thinking or what he was doing."

Megan grimaced. "So, that's a yes?"

Emma laughed. "I was head-over-heels, remember? But I think it's because I knew he would leave one day. And he did."

"He did indeed. Left you a present before he went, though." Megan tapped Emma's stomach.

"You're the only person in the world who could get away with that joke," Emma said.

"I know," Megan replied sweetly.

Over the next few hours, Megan and Emma sat and exchanged stories, ate donuts, and watched television. With Megan by her side to banter with, Emma found the dating shows interesting again, and the two of them spoke to the characters, saying, "Are you really going to wear that tonight?" or, "You don't deserve to kiss the ground she walks on!"

Around dinner time, another few visitors came over: Aunt Cindy, Aunt Elise, Michael's girlfriend, Margot, and Penny, who was visiting her mother from California. In typical dramatic fashion, Penny rushed to Emma's side and said, "Darling, I heard the news. I'm so sorry about everything that's happened to you. I've brought you some tea from a California Healer. This woman knows the ins and outs of the human body in ways traditional medicine doesn't allow."

Emma thanked Penny and put the tea on her bedside table, making a mental note to ask Lily about it before she ingested it. She wasn't sure she trusted "healers" from California.

For the fun of it, Cindy and Tracey set up a table alongside Emma's bed so that everyone could sit around Emma's room for a little party. It was the most fun Emma had had in weeks. It was remarkable to see so many beautiful faces in such a small space.

"Everyone! Tell me what you've been up to," Emma said as they settled, pouring glasses of wine and crunching on chips and pretzels. "Penny? How have your auditions gone?"

Penny swept her long, blonde hair behind her shoulders. "I've nearly gotten three roles so far. My agent thinks my big break is just around the corner."

"Incredible." Emma smiled and lifted her glass of fake wine. "What kinds of roles are you going after?"

"They're all the same," Penny said with a laugh. "I've been

type-casted as the popular girl in teenage high school dramas. Funny to be twenty-three and reading a sixteen-year-old's lines. Then again, I don't think things change so much when you get older."

"What are the storylines?" Megan asked.

"Typical high school stuff. Cheerleading practice. Mean boys. Popularity contests. That kind of thing."

Emma and Megan exchanged glances.

"I know what they're thinking," Tracey interjected. "Growing up on the island was very different. We hardly had enough kids to form a football team, let alone a cheerleading squad."

"Wow. Penny and Brad's high school had thousands of kids," Elise said.

"Suffice it to say, I wasn't the most popular girl in school," Penny explained. "Not like the girls in the scripts I've been reading."

Emma tilted her head, surprised. In her mind, the beautiful and blonde Penny had won every popularity contest she'd ever gone out for. She could picture her as prom queen, cheer captain, and the football quarterback's girlfriend.

Instead, Penny explained it was quite the opposite. "I had braces the entire four years. On top of that, I was obsessed with theater, which isn't exactly cool girl material."

"You couldn't pay me to be a teenager again," Aunt Cindy chimed in. "And I know I had it easier than most. Jeremy and I were in love. I was all right in school. Mom and Dad were generally happy during that time. But still. Sometimes, I would wake up and feel so frightened about what would come next in life. The approaching years seemed insurmountable."

"And yet, we got through them." Tracey squeezed Cindy's hand.

"Barely," Cindy admitted.

The younger women were quiet for a moment, their eyes

downcast. Cindy's great love and the father of her firstborn had passed away in a freak snowmobile accident in his early twenties. After that, Cindy had married Fred, a monster of a man who'd tormented her emotionally for decades. Her life hadn't been easy.

"Let's talk about everyone's favorite topic," Penny interjected, switching the mood. "Uncle Alex is in love!"

Everyone howled with laughter.

"Tell us more about the other night at the Pink Pony, Elise!" Cindy leaned forward, chewing at the edge of a chip. "You have inside information."

"I've never seen him look so happy," Elise said as she stitched her eyebrows together.

"Aw," everyone else echoed.

"But it makes me scared for him," Elise offered. "I remember being freshly divorced and thinking that any new flirtation was the next love of my life. I was disappointed right and left. Until I met Wayne, that is."

"You think we shouldn't trust Lily?" Emma asked, suddenly fearful for her baby all over again.

Elise waved a hand. "I know we've all looked up her midwife qualifications. She's all set on that front."

Everyone around the room nodded. Emma's heart warmed at the due diligence of every female in her circle. They truly cared.

"But romantically? I don't know. Although it's just winter and she doesn't have a date of departure, she is just a tourist. From what I've gleaned, most everyone has gotten their heart broken by a tourist here on Mackinac," Elise continued.

"Including me," Penny sighed. "Last summer was a doozy."

"Alex has hardly ever opened his heart to anyone," Tracey affirmed. "I hope his instincts are right. I hope he's found the right one."

"And if he hasn't?" Cindy breathed.

"We have to find a way to be there for him," Tracey said. "Even though the first thing he'll want to do is cut us out."

"That's his way," Cindy agreed sadly.

After her first glass of wine, Tracey stood quickly and announced she would order pizza for the whole group. Penny began to make a list of pizza orders on her phone. Her face was focused and stoic as she recorded black olives, green peppers, and extra cheese orders in her Notes app. Megan leaned her head on Emma's shoulder and exhaled all the air from her lungs as Emma listened to the vibrant exchanges of her ever-talkative family. In just a couple of weeks (she hoped), they would gather around her baby, hold her baby in their arms, and shroud them both with love. How lucky she was.

Chapter Eight

Alex was at home. This was a rare thing these days, as he spent most nights at the Willow, just in case Lily, Kevin, and Ralphie needed anything. During the day, he tended to the other Swartz properties, babysat Kevin and Ralphie when Lily needed an hour or two to herself, or sat in the Willow office, daydreaming about a future with Lily he wasn't entirely sure would be his. Still, it was so nice to have something to dream about.

Alex's house was a three-bedroom bungalow with too much space for a single man. The wrap-around porch was hardly ever used, and the fireplace was rarely lit. Almost every night he could remember in the place, he'd slept in bed alone. Because of its lack of use, the house was continually spotless. In many ways, it felt like a pretend home, one you toured before you decided to buy.

Now, Alex slipped the last of his clean clothes into his dresser drawers, combed his dark hair in the mirror, donned his winter coat, and stepped into the chilly afternoon. In just a few hours, he would need to begin making dinner for the Willow residents, which required a brief stop at the grocery store. He'd been reading up on gnocchi, and he didn't think it looked too difficult. On top of that, gnocchi had the added benefit of being good for both kids and adults. At least, that was his hope.

Alex walked through downtown Mackinac with a skip to his step. On either side, most of the shop windows were decorated for a Christmas that had already passed. Their owners were away in Florida or Alabama for the harsher winter months and would return in March or April to greet the springtime sun. Alex and his sisters joked they were "weak."

The Grind Coffee Shop was still buzzing, despite the season. Alex stepped into the warmth and inhaled the glorious scent of roasted espresso beans. Michael waved from behind the counter.

"Uncle Alex! You never come in here."

Alex nodded and kicked the snow from his boots. He loved his nephew, although he wasn't sure he fully understood him. So many years after Jeremy's death, Michael looked just like him. He hadn't even been born at the time.

"How are you doing?" Alex asked as he stepped forward.

"Not bad. We just got through a rush. I think I made a thousand low-fat lattes."

"Gross!" Alex tried to laugh, although he still wasn't sure his nephew really understood him, either. "I guess I'll take a regular-fat latte. Oh, and some pastries." He studied the glass case, where chocolate croissants and slices of cake waited expectantly. "Could you box up two slices of cake and four chocolate croissants for me?"

Michael set to work, humming to himself as he prepared Alex's order. Afterward, Alex paid and tipped double what he normally would have, then stepped back outside. A sharp wind crashed into him, but he persevered toward the Willow, deciding to go to the grocery store later instead of now. In only a few moments, he would relax in the warmth before the fire, help Kevin with an art project, and listen to Lily talk about what they'd done that day. Sometimes, she told him about podcasts she'd listened to, ones about science or history. Alex was often too focused on how beautiful and intelligent she was to remember exactly what she said. "That is so fascinating," he said each time. "I can't believe how many interests you have." He genuinely meant it.

Alex stepped into the Willow foyer, placed the latte and the box of pastries and cake on the front desk, and removed his coat.

"Alex?" Kevin's sweet voice came from the seating area.

"Hi, buddy!" Alex headed toward Kevin, where he was all set up with his coloring books, his head bent. "Where's your brother?"

"He's asleep upstairs," Kevin explained.

"And your mom?"

Kevin shrugged and continued to color. Alex glanced around the room for some sign of her and found her computer on the table with her slippers next to the couch. She couldn't have gone far.

For a little while, Alex sat on the couch and looked at his phone, content to wait for her to return. But when she wasn't back five minutes later, he grew anxious. He hustled upstairs to look for her, but the suite was dark with Ralphie sleeping soundly in his toddler bed. Back downstairs, he paused at the front desk and realized his office door was open just a crack.

Had he left it open? That wasn't like him. He was very organized, and his sisters had been relentless in teasing him about it over the years.

Was it possible that Lily was in there? No. It didn't make any sense. Why would she enter his office, his private domain, and the place where he kept all important documents?

Slowly, dreading the worst, Alex tip-toed toward the

cracked door. His heart pounded as he pressed his face through the crack.

There, standing at his desk, was Lily. Her face didn't look like the one he knew. Rather, she was stoic and serious, poring over documents, her finger scanning line after line. Several folders were spread open before her.

Alex wanted to turn back. He wanted to run out of the Willow and come back in again to find a completely different scene. *This had to be another dimension, right? This couldn't be happening.*

From the door, Alex's voice boomed. "What do you think you're doing?"

Lily froze. Her eyes were enormous. For a long moment, they stared at each other like a predator and its prey in the forest. Afterward, she began to close all the folders and stuff them back into the shelf beside the desk.

"I'm sorry! It's not what it looks like," she cried.

Alex was flabbergasted. No, more than that, he was angry. He stepped through the door, watching as she tidied the folders. Her eyes were rimmed with red. His silence terrified her. It scared him, too. He wasn't sure what he planned to say.

"You need to get out of my office." He sounded awful.

Lily's eyes filled with tears. "Please. Will you let me explain?"

Alex stepped forward. His arms shook violently, so he crossed them over his chest. "I don't want to hear your explanation. I don't want to talk. I've seen enough!"

Lily's lips parted with surprise. "Alex, please. It's so complicated."

"What could be complicated about you going through personal files and documents?" Alex demanded. He was reminded of over a year ago when Elise had come snooping around the island. He'd thought she was up to no good, but he'd never caught her doing anything as damaging as this.

"I can't believe I trusted you," he blared. "Get out!"

Lily rushed from behind the desk and hustled past him. She brushed his hand accidentally on her way to Kevin. Once there, she scooped him up, eyeing Alex angrily. *Why should she be angry? She'd overstepped every boundary.* Probably, she'd flirted with him just to get closer to the files in the first place. Shame made Alex's cheeks burn. He stepped toward her, watching as she hustled for the staircase with Kevin in her arms.

"Alex?" Kevin smiled sweetly from Lily's embrace.

Alex's heart cracked into pieces. It hadn't been long since Lily, and the boys had stumbled into his life. Had she known he was so vulnerable? Had she put her kids in his care to manipulate him? *What was her goal?*

It didn't matter. Alex was too terrified to know the depths of her game.

"I need you out of the Willow by the end of the week," Alex said, his tone ominous.

Lily stalled on the staircase but didn't turn around. Kevin did, peering over her shoulder. His curls were a mess. Alex thought of the recipe for gnocchi, about how he planned to ask Lily, Kevin, and Ralphie if they wanted to go to the grocery store with him. Such a banal task was always more fun with the ones you loved.

Before Lily could answer, Alex turned on his heel and stomped back into his office. He shivered with anger. On the other side of his desk, he began to go through the file folders for some understanding of what she was looking for. But the files covered so many different elements of the business. Many of them were incomprehensible unless you worked in hospitality. *Was Lily not a midwife, after all? Or was there something more complex about her situation— something that couldn't be seen from the surface?*

For the hundredth time, Alex pulled up Lily's midwife

website, which outlined her commitment to her clients and their babies. A number of women had given reviews of Lily's services. One of them, a woman named Gretchen Sommers, had given Lily four stars out of five. *Why only four?* Alex looked up Gretchen Sommers' number in the online white pages and soon found himself calling her, feeling like a spy.

"Hello?" A young woman answered the phone.

Alex stuttered. "Uh, hi. My name is Alex Swartz, and my wife is about to have a baby. We're looking for a midwife and have been reading up on Lily Franklin. I noticed you only gave her a four-star rating, while the others gave her a five-star. Can you tell me why?"

In the background, a little kid could be heard talking. Gretchen shushed him and said she would be right there. "Mommy's on the phone." After that, there was another pause before she continued. "Lily Franklin was my midwife for all three of my pregnancies," she explained.

"Oh, wow. Three children!"

"Quite a handful," Gretchen said.

"You must have liked Lily's work?"

"I really did." Gretchen paused. "The four-star rating was probably because my husband got into a fight with her husband. During my third delivery, her husband came to find her. He was drunk and belligerent and started screaming her name outside. It was really distracting. Actually, it felt dangerous."

Alex's heart pounded. *This was strange.*

"I heard through the grapevine that they're not together anymore," Gretchen continued. "Which means I should really ask Lily if I can change my review. I feel bad about that. I wouldn't want anyone to think Lily wasn't a stellar midwife just because of my four-star review."

"You were angry. I can understand that."

"Thanks. Well. Listen. Go with Lily. She's remarkable. She

brought my babies into the world, and they're happy and healthy. I owe her everything."

Alex got off the phone and continued to read the reviews, all of which were stellar. He then studied Lily's social media accounts for some sign of who she really was. In most photographs, she carried one or both of her children and smiled next to friends or relatives. A few further back in her timeline showed her with a handsome man with the same dark curls Kevin had. This had to be her ex-husband. *Why had he shown up drunk outside Gretchen's labor? What had he been screaming about?*

Alex's head thudded with questions. Beyond anything, he knew he couldn't fully trust Lily— not now that he'd discovered her going through his things. This broke his heart more than anything. Despite knowing it was the wrong thing to do, he'd hung all of his hopes and dreams upon Lily and her boys, praying for the future he'd always yearned for. Now, it was completely gone.

Chapter Nine

Emma's next appointment with Lily was set for that Friday at noon. Megan was over as usual, typing through a college essay in the corner of Emma's room while Emma read a romance novel. In the kitchen, Tracey continued to fight through the last of her boutique orders, creating a tower of packages that Megan reported was as tall as Arch Rock. "Tourists will come and take pictures in front of it if it stays there too long," Megan joked.

When Lily rang the doorbell, Megan ran off to get it, saying she couldn't focus anyway. Emma set her book to the side and mentally prepared herself for another session with Lily. The questions she wanted to ask— like, *when would the baby come?* — were useless. Lily didn't know. Nobody did. It was the waiting game of the year.

"Hi, there!" Tracey greeted Lily. Afterward came the squeal of Lily's two children, followed by the stomping of their little feet.

"I hope you don't mind I brought the boys," Lily said sheepishly.

"We don't mind at all," Megan said. "I'm surprised Alex couldn't watch them."

"Oh, he has so much work to get caught up on. We've taken up too much of his time already," Lily insisted.

"It's the winter season," Tracey scoffed. "Whatever work he has, he's made up for himself."

Emma watched as Lily and Tracey walked down the hallway toward her bedroom. Lily looked slightly tired around the eyes, as though she hadn't slept well. She carried a large duffel bag and announced the supplies for the birth had arrived. "We're all set," she said. "Now, we just wait for your little baby to decide to join us."

In the living room, Kevin and Ralphie giggled madly at something Megan was doing. Emma's heart lifted. She wished she could see her cousin play with the kids. It made her think of the way Megan would be with her own child— open-hearted and eager to laugh.

As Lily set up, she said, "Downtown is gorgeous right now. That extra snowfall last night makes everything so picturesque. And there are little stalls set up on either side of Main Street and along the docks. Is there something going on?"

Tracey and Emma exchanged smiles.

"It's the Winter Festival!" Emma exclaimed. "I almost forgot."

"It happens every year," Tracey continued. "There are so many events all day long. I suppose this morning, already, they had the snowmobile race over the ice. But in a little while, all those stalls will open to sell mulled wine, beer, baked goods, and chili. All the islanders bundle up and gather together all day long."

"It's a wonderful day," Emma said with a sigh. "I can't believe I have to miss it this year."

Lily's lips formed an O. "I think Alex mentioned this

festival a few days ago. Is it true your sister Cindy lost her boyfriend there?"

Tracey's eyes were shadowed with sorrow. "It was a horrible day. A complete accident. Now, everyone is extra-careful about the ice. There hasn't been a bad accident like that since."

"Thank goodness," Lily said.

It was bizarre, Emma thought, that Lily already knew so many of their family stories. She knew about Cindy's loss. She knew that Emma planned to raise her baby with her mother. Probably, she even knew about Grandpa Dean's affair, the act that had splintered Alex's heart.

After Emma's check-up, Lily sat back down on the chair beside Emma's bed. In the next room, Kevin howled with laughter as Megan performed animal noises. *Was she a monkey? A lion?* It was difficult to say.

"You should really take the kids down to the Winter Festival." Tracey returned to the bedroom with a mug of tea for Lily. "Emma always loved it when she was little."

"I still love it," Emma breathed. "I hate that I can't go this year."

Lily tilted her head. Her eyes glistened. "You know what? Why don't we get you there?"

"What are you talking about?" Emma laughed. She hadn't seen anything but the four walls of her room in ages.

"I mean, just because you're on bed rest, doesn't mean we can't transport that bed." Lily turned to face Tracey, who looked just as confused as Emma felt. "Do you have anything flat and on wheels? Anything we could place a mattress on?"

"I have this cart for the boutique orders," Tracey said excitedly. "Maybe we could put the spare mattress on the cart? Line it with blankets and pillows?"

"Mom. It's too crazy," Emma said, although her heart had begun to lift.

"We'll have to take it nice and slow," Lily affirmed. "And avoid cobblestones."

"Of course." Tracey jumped from her chair and called for Megan. "Meg! We're going to need your help."

"It's outrageous," Emma interjected, although she already sensed there was no turning back.

"If you get cold or uncomfortable at any time, we can always come back," Tracey told Emma.

"Cold? Who do you think I am?" Emma demanded. "I'm a Mackinac girl. I know there's no bad weather. Just bad clothing."

Within the hour, Emma's makeshift bed on wheels was ready to go. The biggest issue was getting Emma onto the wheeling bed itself. To do this, Lily helped Emma walk gently to the hallway, where the cart awaited. She positioned herself on the mattress and wiggled into the middle, where Megan collected piles of blankets around her.

"You're like the winter queen," Megan teased.

"Wow!" Kevin hustled to the side of the cart and blinked up at Emma. "What are you doing up there?"

"I can't walk right now," Emma explained. "And your momma figured out how I could go to the festival, anyway."

"Wow," Kevin repeated.

"She's pretty special," Tracey said, beaming at Lily.

Lily's cheek twitched. Again, Emma had the feeling she was severely underslept. As Tracey and Megan hunted for their coats, Emma whispered, "Lily, are you okay?"

Lily locked eyes with Emma for a moment. "I'm just fine, honey. I'm glad we can all go to the festival together. You're all so blessed to have one another. I hope you know that."

With Megan and Tracey handling the cart and Lily handling her children, they set out from the house very slowly. Soft snow melted across Emma's cheeks, and the bright light of the sun filtered through the clouds, making the snow-lined rooftops glimmer. Emma had never been cooped up inside for so long. Only now that she was out in the fresh air did she recognize how crazy she'd felt.

The Winter Festival was off to a wonderful start. Mackinac residents and tourists who'd braved the cold wandered the snow-lined streets, drinking mulled wine, eating warm food and sweets, and gossiping. Tracey and Megan wheeled Emma's cart not far from the chili and mulled wine stands. There, they propped the cart up so that Emma could take in the entire scene comfortably.

"Are you warm enough?" Tracey asked Emma.

Emma laughed. "I have five blankets wrapped around me. I think I'm good."

"Do you want hot chocolate, Kevin?" Lily squatted down to adjust Kevin's winter coat. "What about you, Ralphie?"

Both boys squealed with excitement.

"I think that means yes," Lily said. "Will you girls be okay by yourselves?"

"We won't get into too much trouble," Megan said, waving as both Lily and Tracey disappeared into the crowd to get supplies.

"This is crazy," Emma said, giggling as Megan perched next to her on the cart and dug under the blankets.

"We were born and raised here. Probably everyone here who's older than us saw us running around in diapers. This is just another phase of your beautiful and very different island life. Embrace it!" Megan smiled.

In the crowd, they watched as Tracey ordered mulled wine and hot chocolate, plus three orders of chili. One of the workers navigated the crowd with her to deliver the chili. He laughed at Emma's set-up and said, "You always knew how to travel in style, Emma."

Emma accepted the bowl of chili and thanked him. "I'll be doing this every year from now on."

"Genius," the worker said, shaking his head as he returned to the chili stand.

"I got you hot chocolate with extra marshmallows," Tracey explained as she passed Emma the drink. "I know how cold weather makes you want to eat your weight in sugar."

"Actually, I think that's due to the pregnancy," Emma joked.

"I can't wait to be pregnant," Megan quipped as she lifted her mulled wine. "Will you promise to get pregnant again so we can do it together?"

Emma howled with laughter. "You better be joking."

Megan feigned seriousness. "Why would I be joking?"

"All right. If I ever go on a date again, and I fall in love and decide to have a child with someone on purpose, I promise I will try to work with your pregnancy schedule."

"That's all I ask."

Soon after, Lily returned with her children, some mulled wine, and a cup of hot chocolate for the boys to share.

"There's a snowman-building competition?" she asked.

"That's right. And Megan and I were defeated terribly one year," Emma said.

"Oh gosh. I remember. We were so convinced we were going to win, and then our snowman's head fell off."

Lily closed her eyes and wheezed with laughter. "I wish I could have grown up in a place like this. So many traditions! So many memories!"

"There's no reason you can't stay," Emma heard herself say.

Lily looked deflated. She dropped down to help Ralphie first, then watched Kevin sip a bit of hot chocolate. Then, she took a long drink from her mulled wine.

"Hello, all!" A very bundled-up Marcy and Kurt stepped through the crowd to greet them. They walked hand-in-hand, completely in love.

"Marcy! A rare thing to see you at the Winter Festival," Tracey said.

"Kurt dragged me out. Told me to stop being such a Grinch." Marcy smiled up at Kurt. "Besides, it's hard to say no to mulled wine."

"She refuses to go ice skating with me," Kurt explained.

"It's just because I don't want to embarrass you." Marcy winked.

After Marcy and Kurt returned to the crowd to grab another mug of hot wine, Tracey turned to Lily and asked, "Why don't you invite Alex down here? He never comes to the Winter Festival. It would do him good."

Lily blinked several times. Emma sipped her hot chocolate, realizing her mother had stepped over an invisible boundary.

"I'm sorry," Tracey stuttered. "I just thought..."

"It's okay. It's my fault. Alex is angry with me. Really, really angry."

Tracey rolled her eyes slightly. "That's just Alex. He's stubborn. He doesn't always have the best instincts when it comes to people. But he genuinely means well."

Lily locked eyes with Tracey. She looked stoic and serious. "There's no way to repair what happened."

Her words were final.

"Mommy!" Kevin grabbed Lily's pants and tugged, pointing with his free hand toward a group of toddlers playing in the snow.

"You want to play with those kids?" Lily asked sweetly. She then lifted Ralphie into her arms, nodded back to the Swartz women, and guided Kevin to the group.

This, of course, left the Swartz women time to gossip.

"Oh. I feel so sad!" Tracey sighed. "I really thought Alex had found someone."

"He can be so difficult," Megan said.

"I wonder what happened?" Emma asked.

"It could have been anything," Megan tried.

"Maybe he got cold feet," Tracey muttered. "We should tell her to keep trying. Maybe it'll snap some sense into him."

"She is just a tourist, though," Emma offered. "Maybe it's for the best, so he doesn't get his heart broken?"

Emma, Tracey, and Megan sipped their warm drinks, watching as Lily squatted next to her children in the snow, rolling snowballs in her gloved hands and making them giggle. In every sense, she seemed the perfect woman. *What was Alex's problem?*

Chapter Ten

Alex sat alone in his living room with a mug of hot chocolate. Several blocks away, the Mackinac Island Winter Festival finished out, the evening casting a chill through the air that sent even the strongest Mackinac residents back home. His heart felt very dark. For years, he'd found a way to ignore his loneliness, yet now, it jumped up to bite him, to scream in his ears that he would never be enough.

Over and over again, Alex had run the incident at the Willow through his mind. Still, he hadn't gotten up the courage to go to Lily's room to ask her why on earth she'd been going through his files. On the one hand, he was quite angry. But on the other, he was embarrassed that he'd acted so outrageously. What kind of man didn't pause, wait, and listen? A stubborn one. It was just as his sisters always said. He was stubborn, above all. And he was going to die alone because of it.

Alex stood, walked to the kitchen, and hunted through his cabinets for something to eat. There was a package of pasta and a container of sauce. This was food meant for lonely men who didn't feel up to cooking a big meal for just one person.

Alex placed a large pot of water on the stovetop. In one of the fancy glasses, he poured himself a glass of red wine and put on a podcast about French history, wondering if Lily had ever listened to it. He'd once adored history, but that had been long before he'd given his life to his work. Why had he given up on learning things? *Wasn't there so much to know?*

Even before the water had begun to boil, there was a knock at the door. This was a rare thing in Alex's life. In fact, he couldn't remember the last time he'd had someone over. He hustled to the foyer and opened the door to discover not one but three people: Tracey, Cindy, and Elise.

"Hello, Alex!" They sang it all together. Elise fit in with his other sisters with perfection. *How did she do it? Had she always fit in so easily?*

"Wow. Hi." Alex rubbed the back of his head nervously. "To what do I owe the pleasure?"

Their cheeks were bright pink, either from chill or drinking mulled wine or a bit of both.

"We were just at the Winter Festival," Tracey confessed. "And couldn't help but notice you weren't around."

"When was the last time I went to the Winter Festival?" Alex asked.

Elise laughed tipsily. "Emma was there. They wheeled her in a cart all the way downtown. She and Megan were so cozy under blankets."

Alex smiled, imagining the scene. "You could have invited me, you know."

Elise, Tracey, and Cindy exchanged nervous glances. They realized they'd made a mistake.

"Well, we're inviting you out now," Cindy chimed in. "We want to get some dinner and hit up the Pink Pony. What do you say?"

Alex lifted his thumb toward the kitchen. "I'm making dinner, actually."

"What's for dinner?" Elise asked.

Alex paused for a beat.

"It's pasta. Isn't it, Alex?" Tracey giggled.

Alex rolled his eyes but didn't say no.

"Alex! You can eat some crappy pasta every other day of your life. Come out with your sisters. You never come out with us," Cindy urged.

Alex wanted to protest. He wanted to tell them that, actually, the reason he never came out was because he wasn't invited. Instead, he rolled his eyes a final time and told them, "Fine. Let me go turn off the stove." In a flash, he had his coat, hat, and gloves on, and he was out the door. It was time.

Out on Main Street, Alex fell into an easy stride with his three sisters. He loved the sound of their voices and laughter, ricocheting from building to building. He loved feeling a part of them, if only for tonight.

Together, they grabbed burritos, sitting together at a small table near the window. Alex's chicken and black bean burrito was monstrous and delicious, seasoned with a spicy green sauce. It was miles better than any pasta.

Because they were tipsy, Elise, Tracey, and Cindy ate sloppily, needing plenty of napkins. Alex fetched a big pile, teasing them.

"You're like college students!"

"That's a great compliment. Isn't it, girls?" Tracey laughed and dabbed her lips with her napkin.

"Yes. Please, Alex. Keep telling us how young we look!" Elise cried.

After burritos, they grabbed their coats and hustled down the block to the Pink Pony. Many Winter Festival revelers had taken refuge there and now sipped beers or wine, laughing after the beautiful insanity of the day or watching the television screens. College students played basketball or hockey, throwing themselves across the court and rink. Behind the bar, Marcy and Kurt filled beer after beer, chatting to customers with big, loving smiles.

The Swartz siblings grabbed a table in the corner, and Kurt poured Alex's beer and the three women's wine. When everyone had a glass, they raised them in the center and cheered another successful Winter Festival.

"How is Emma feeling?" Alex asked as they settled in.

"She's very uncomfortable and bored," Tracey admitted.

"These are her last days of boredom," Elise offered.

"I told her that, but I don't think it really helps," Tracey said. She then side-eyed Alex and added, "Lily's been a tremendous help. Emma always lights up when she comes over. To be honest, it calms both of us down to know someone is watching out for Emma's health here on the island. I'm not sure what we would have done otherwise."

Alex sniffed and sipped his beer.

"She seems like such a great woman," Elise chimed in. "I loved talking to her the other night at the Pink Pony."

"Her little boys are so adorable," Cindy added. "It must be hard for her to be a single mother. I only did it for a little while with Michael, and it nearly destroyed me."

Alex's cheeks burned with fear and embarrassment. He had the sudden hunch that his sisters had dragged him out to the bar to pepper him with questions about Lily. They were the ultimate meddlers.

"Don't you just love those little boys, Alex?" Cindy asked.

"Yeah. Kevin and Ralphie are fantastic." Alex fluffed his hair and kept his eyes straight ahead.

"You looked so happy playing with them at our place," Tracey said.

"It's fun." Alex didn't want to give anything away.

Elise, Cindy, and Tracey sipped their wine and exchanged glances. Alex willed himself to drink the rest of his beer and run back home, where he could sit in the silence of himself. No one would pester him there.

"I mean, aren't you going to take Lily out on another date?" Tracey demanded. She was always the more impatient sister.

Alex rolled his eyes. "Here we go."

"What is your problem?" Cindy asked. "You've finally met a woman who seems to really like you!"

"Gee. Thanks."

"That's not what I mean." Cindy sounded exasperated.

"What she means is, we think you seemed really happy with Lily. And we really like seeing you happy." Elise was more diplomatic. She had to be, as the half-sister.

"Well, I wasn't happy." Alex's voice was stiff.

"That's baloney," Tracey said. She smashed her fist into the center of the table. "Lily says you're mad at her. What could she have possibly done to make you so angry? Because, Alex, if you don't loosen your rules around how people are allowed to act around you, I don't think you're going to get anywhere."

The words were harsh. They stung Alex's cheek as though he'd been smacked. Rage boiled over, and soon, he found himself saying what he hadn't wanted to.

"If you must know, I found Lily in the back office of the Willow." Alex seethed. "She was going through documents. Tearing everything apart, as though she was looking for something."

At this, Elise, Tracey, and Cindy looked at each other in shock.

"Are you sure?" Cindy gasped.

Alex raised his hands. "I know what I saw."

"But that's ridiculous. What could she have been looking for?" Elise demanded. "She's a tourist on the island."

"Spoken by someone who came to this island looking for her father," Alex pointed out.

Elise's eyes dropped.

Tracey's face transformed. "My gosh. Should we fire her?"

Alex grumbled. "No. I don't think so. I made some phone calls about her work as a midwife. She seems totally legitimate in that regard." For some reason, he left out the story about her emotionally abusive ex-husband. He just didn't want to go into it.

"Did you ask her what she was looking for?" Elise asked.

Alex stiffened.

"Alex!" Tracey sighed.

"It's too late," Alex blared. "She crossed my boundaries. Worse, she crossed our family business's boundaries. I can't trust her after that."

Suddenly, Marcy appeared at their table. Her face was stony.

"We're all right on drinks, Marcy," Alex said quickly.

But Marcy remained. "I couldn't help but overhear."

"Does this mean we'll be a part of the gossip circuit from now on?" Alex demanded, throwing her an icy glare.

Marcy crossed her arms over her chest. "Calm down, Alex Swartz. You're always jumping to conclusions, aren't you? But no. I've come here to say you can absolutely trust that young woman, Lily. She seems to be a remarkable human being. Someone I would trust with my life."

"How on earth do you know that?" Alex asked.

"I won't go into details," Marcy said. "All I can say is this. She came to the island to look for answers about her family, just like some of you here at this very table." She stared at Elise, who nodded. "I would hope you could offer her a bit more compassion than most."

"What about her family?" Alex pushed her.

But Marcy shook her head. "I've already said too much. But your sisters are right, Alex. You need to loosen up on your expectations of people. Take it from me. I was alone for thirty-five years. If I could go back and tell myself to try to learn to be happy, I would."

After that, she turned on a heel, traipsed behind the bar, and kissed Kurt on the cheek. "What was that for?" Kurt asked, his voice hardly heard over the bar crowd.

"Wow. I wonder what she's looking for?" Elise asked, swirling the wine in her glass.

Tracey reached across the table and took Alex's hand. Her eyes were urgent. "I think you need to go back to the Willow and get to the bottom of this. At worst, Lily is in some kind of trouble. She's alone with two young boys. She's going to need your help."

Alex stuttered. This new knowledge had given him whiplash. Was it possible he could trust Lily, after all? He sucked down the rest of his beer, feeling outside of himself.

"Go get her," Elise said firmly.

Alex fumbled for his wallet, but his sisters shooed him out of the bar. He soon found himself in the sharp chill of the night with his red nose pointed toward the Willow. There, Lily was probably still up, her heart aching for reasons Alex could not know. He needed to get to the bottom of it. This was his only hope.

Chapter Eleven

A fire crackled in the sitting area, reflecting its light across the bay window. Lily was tucked beneath a blanket, a book spread across her lap. A few toys were strewn across the carpet in front of her, but it was late, so the boys were upstairs, asleep. Alex closed the front door quietly and entered the sitting area. The chill from his coat beamed off of him. Lily stirred and turned her face toward his. Her eyes were wounded.

"Hi," Alex said.

"Hi." Slowly, she closed her book and turned to stare into the fire. After a long pause, she said, "The boys and I had quite a day. They loved the Winter Festival. I think I gave them too much sugar, though. Getting them to bed was painful."

Alex tried to laugh, but it sounded all wrong. He dropped himself into the chair across from her and watched the fire, as well. The tension between them was striking. It made it difficult to breathe.

"Listen, Alex. I don't want to fight with you." Lily sounded so tired and sad. Alex's heart cracked at the edges.

"I don't want to fight with you, either."

Lily's eyes lifted toward his. She looked surprised.

"You really caught me off guard," Alex explained timidly. "I couldn't understand why you would be in my office like that. And because I've been disappointed and lied to over and over again in my life, I just assumed you were the next person to do that."

Lily nodded. "Thank you for saying that." She paused, then added, "But it's true. I shouldn't have been going through your stuff. You created such a beautiful and cozy environment for the kids and I, and I totally disrespected you."

It was Alex's turn to be surprised. It was a rare thing that he dealt with adults who were so emotionally aware. Hesitantly, he leaned forward, yearning again to kiss her. But there was so much he had to understand first.

"I'm really sorry I didn't let you explain yourself. Would you mind trying to, now?"

Lily sighed and wrapped herself tighter in the blanket. She suddenly looked much older than her mid-thirties, as though stress and sorrow had stamped their way across her face. Alex could relate. He sometimes looked much older than his age, as well.

"I think I told you I've been separated from my husband for about a year," Lily offered. "He wasn't exactly the nicest guy in the world. Every single one of my girlfriends warned me about him before we had kids. Then again, I was completely in love with him— and you can't reason with anyone who is so in love."

Alex nodded along, although he'd never been so in love. He couldn't relate.

"After one especially terrible fight, I kicked him out of the house, and he started paying child support. Despite his normal tendencies to manipulate and scheme, we had a pretty decent arrangement. He saw the kids about two or three times a week, always under my supervision. He was also trying pretty hard to get me back. I thought about it a few times. I mean, I always pictured my life with a partner, raising our children in a cozy house with a picket fence. I hadn't been allowed that as a kid, and I was pretty sure it was the only way to happiness."

"It makes sense," Alex offered. "It's the kind of happiness you deserve."

"Thank you for saying that." Lily looked pained. "Now, this is where things get foggy for me. In the summertime, my brother came to Mackinac Island to do seasonal work. He told me it was a common thing. That he could work really hard for a few months and make a lot of money."

"It is," Alex confirmed. "The island's population booms from May to September and then whittles down to nothing. There is a lot of money to be made if you're in the right field."

Lily nodded, furrowing her brow. "I'm not sure exactly what he did. Boat work, maybe. Handyman stuff. Occasionally, my husband came up to visit my brother. I have no idea what they did up here. Probably, they did a lot of things I don't want to know about. Before we met, my husband was something of a playboy, and I'm pretty sure my brother is no different. Don't get me wrong. I love him. He's family. But he can be a piece of work."

"That's family for you."

Lily smiled sadly. "Toward the end of summer, I stopped hearing from my brother. I called his phone number over and over again for a week or two, but it always went straight to voicemail. When I went to the police about it, they laughed at me and said my brother was an adult. If he wanted to disappear, he could do as he pleased."

"That's terrible," Alex breathed.

"Around this time, my ex-husband was supposed to come by to hang out with the kids. He didn't show up. I called him, and I got his voicemail. It was like déjà vu."

Alex's eyes widened. "You're kidding."

"I wish I was." Lily sniffed and curled her hair around her ears. She spoke too quickly, as though she needed to get the entire story out at once. "Since that day in August, I haven't heard a peep out of my brother or my ex-husband. I don't know where they are. I don't know what they've gotten themselves into. I don't know if they concocted some scheme to get away from me."

"Why would your brother want to get away from you?" Alex asked.

Lily shook her head. "I wish I knew. I really do. I was nothing but good to my brother. I gave him a place to stay when he needed it. I gave him money when I had it."

The story was shocking. Alex stood and paced behind his chair, trying to make sense of it.

"I spent the first few months in a strange state," Lily continued. "I had to keep my children and I above water, so I took a second job at the hospital. I reached out to all of my brother's friends and all of our extended family. I even called my ex-husband's mother— a woman I really don't like— to see if she'd heard from him. No lead led me anywhere. It was disheartening, to say the least."

"I can't even imagine."

Lily's eyes lifted toward Alex's. "Christmas was the last straw. I felt so alone in that little house with my babies. Ralphie was sick again— like always, as you've seen. And Kevin only had a few toys to play with. I know I need to organize myself better. I need to start working again as a midwife. I need to make goals. But each time I try, I feel so stunted. Where on earth did my baby's father go? Where is my brother? And why did they abandon me like this?"

Alex hurried around the chair, unable to keep away from her. He collapsed beside her and wrapped his arms around her. Every instinct he had told him to project Lily. This woman was damaged, sure that anyone she got close to was just about to abandon her. He had to prove he never would, even if that meant they could only be friends.

"Listen to me," Alex whispered.

Lily turned her head slightly to peer into his eyes.

"You didn't deserve this. Do you understand?"

Lily lowered her eyebrows.

"I know I haven't known you long. But from what I can tell, you're kind, considerate, funny, and intelligent. Your husband sounds like an abuser. Your brother sounds like a flake. I'm not saying they're not deserving of love because, deep down, everyone is."

Lily swallowed. She looked flabbergasted. "I should have told you all of this from the beginning, huh?"

"It would have made things a whole lot easier." Alex laughed. He felt like he was floating.

Lily lifted her head and kissed him gently on the cheek. Warmth flowed through him. He nearly kissed her on the lips after that but managed to stop himself. This wasn't the time.

"But wait a minute." He shook his head. "Why were you going through my office?"

Lily's eyes clouded. "I spoke to my brother just a few times over the summer. He mentioned he'd picked up some work here at the Willow. I wanted to find his work records. I thought maybe he'd included a forwarding address for tax purposes."

"He worked here?" Alex was surprised. "Do you know what he did?"

Lily shook her head. "I don't. And honestly, I don't think he was here for long. It was just the only lead I had."

"You already asked Marcy about your brother?"

"Yes. I heard she knew everything about everybody here on the island. She'd seen my brother around and heard he'd worked as a handyman for a ferry boat company. Unfortunately, that ferry company closed its doors this autumn. The phone just rings and rings with no answer. I have no idea how to get a hold of them."

"Ah. Yeah. Arnold Line closed up," Alex explained. "And their owners took off for Florida."

Lily grimaced. "That's what I was afraid of."

"Let's look at the records here," Alex said. He stood from the cozy couch, already missing the heat from her body. "Come on."

Lily followed after him, her foot falls soft against the carpeting. When they reached the office, Alex flicked on the lights and walked toward his computer, explaining that most everything regarding employees was kept online these days.

"I should have known," Lily tried to joke. "Technological advancements are not helpful for a girl who wants to snoop."

"Not unless you can guess my password," Alex joked back.

"Hmm. Hey Alex? I was just thinking about my very first childhood pet. Did you have one? And what was its name?"

"Ha. Ha." Alex quickly typed his password and entered the system. Lily gave him her brother's name, and he found the file easily, which included a photograph, an address, and a phone number.

"Looks like he worked in the kitchen here at the Willow for two and a half weeks," Alex said. "It was the first half of July, which is a crazy time for us."

"I take it you don't recognize him?"

"We hired so many temporary staff members during that time. Plus, Dad and I had to manage all the other properties over the summer. I was only here about twice a week."

"Shoot."

"What about this address?" Alex clicked through to make her brother's street address larger.

"No." Lily looked deflated. "That's his address back in Detroit. He hasn't been there at all since he left for Mackinac."

Alex sighed and dropped onto his office chair. He suddenly ached to fix this problem for Lily. *But how?*

"That might be the end of the line," Lily said.

"There has to be another way to figure out what happened to him," Alex muttered. "There has to be a trail."

He suddenly felt like a detective on a crime show. If Lily's brother had worked at the Willow for two weeks last July and for the Arnold Ferry Line sometime over the summer, people on the island had either known him or seen him in passing.

"Will you let me help you?" Alex asked softly. He didn't want to overstep.

Lily pressed her lips together. She seemed the sort of woman unaccustomed to accepting help.

"I know almost everyone on this island," Alex coaxed. "I can try to get to the bottom of this. If you'll let me."

Lily perched at the edge of his desk. The tension between them had doubled— but it was no longer filled with anger. She wanted him, maybe as much as Alex wanted her. It was thrilling.

"Okay, Alex. I'll let you help me."

Chapter Twelve

Alex's mission was set. That night, after Lily kissed him on the lips with her eyes closed, he stayed up long past midnight, hunting for some sign of Lily's brother on social media. Unfortunately, he hadn't updated any of his photos or posted anything since early summer on Mackinac. Several photos featured him in an Arnold Ferry uniform. In one, he hoisted a big suitcase on his shoulder and grinned at the camera— a man in his late twenties with the world at his feet. In another, he was at one of the beach bonfires on the other side of the island, the ones frequented by twenty-somethings who drank domestic beer and stayed up all night long. As a twenty-something, Alex had very rarely been invited to those parties.

The next morning, underslept and raggedy, Alex made breakfast for Lily and the boys, then helped Lily bundle them up for a brisk walk to Arch Rock. As Kevin and Ralphie bounced through the snow, Lily and Alex stood a bit away, holding hands and talking softly about their plan to find Lily's brother. Beside them, the frozen lake stretched out from the beach, shining beneath the winter sun.

"My dad has a contact at Arnold Ferry Line," Alex explained as they gathered the boys to return to the Willow. "He sent me the details this morning. I'll make a few calls and see what I find."

"You're amazing," Lily said, her eyes alight.

With the boys upstairs napping and Lily wrapped in a blanket for a rest of her own, Alex entered his office to call the previous assistant manager at Arnold Ferry Line. When the man answered, Alex spoke in an overly-friendly way.

"Hi, Hank! I don't know if we've ever been introduced. My name is Alex Swartz. I'm the son of Dean Swartz here on Mackinac."

"Oh yes. I'm familiar with you, Alex." Hank didn't sound pleased. "Your father texted me this morning, saying to expect a call from you. Great man, your father. I always liked him."

"Ah. Okay. Yeah, he is." Alex paused, dwelling in sorrow. Everyone always liked his dad so much more than him. "Is now a bad time to talk?"

"It's as good a time as any. I'm in Mississippi, working in hospitality. I'm on a break."

"Must be nice down there."

"It's okay."

Alex was fidgety. "I have a question about a previous employee of yours at Arnold."

"Oh, jeez. Do you know how many employees we dealt with last summer alone?"

Alex understood, but he had to try. His voice was panicked as he gave Hank Lily's brother's name and did his best to describe him. "Late twenties. Broad-shouldered. There's a possibility that he also did handyman work, maybe something mechanical with the boats."

"That name doesn't ring a bell," Hank said. "I'm sorry. I don't think I can be of any help."

"Do you have another employee's number? Someone who might have known him?"

"I can't just give out previous employees' numbers," Hank barked back. "Now, if you'll excuse me. My break is over."

The call was cut.

Alex slumped over in his office chair. Anger swelled in his chest. Yet again, he questioned his own lack of social skills. If only people on the island liked and respected him the way they did his father. Maybe then, he might have been friendly with Hank in the past. Maybe then, he would have even crossed paths with Lily's brother and been able to help her.

Later that night, as Lily put her sons to bed, Alex donned his winter coat and headed for the Pink Pony. It was now February, and a large bouquet of roses sat on the bar top. Marcy hustled across the still-empty bar to hide them.

"Kurt's insisted on celebrating Valentine's Day every single day of February," she said, blushing. "He's a sap." Still, she dropped her nose into the roses and closed her eyes. She looked beautiful.

Alex slid onto a stool at the bar top and ordered a beer. For a little while, Marcy was in the back doing inventory, and he watched the television screens, trying to make sense of a game sort of like pool called snooker. By the time Marcy returned, he'd almost gotten it.

"Some game, huh?" Alex had never been great at small talk.

"Oh yeah. You want to change it?" Marcy grabbed the remote control and turned to go through the channels. "I never know what the guests want to watch. I usually wait till someone complains, then make them feel guilty for complaining." She gave Alex a wry grin.

"You're tough, Marcy." Alex laughed.

Marcy returned the television to snooker, then turned to wash a few beer glasses.

"Marcy? Can I ask you something?" Alex's voice wavered dangerously.

Marcy cocked her head. "I don't suppose this has anything to do with Lily. I told you already. I don't want to meddle in her business."

"She told me about her missing brother and ex-husband," Alex interjected.

Marcy's face calmed. "I see."

"And I want to help her track them down. It's crazy they abandoned her like that."

"It certainly is."

"When Marcy asked you about her brother, did you know who he was?" Alex asked.

Marcy nodded. "He came in here a few times, usually with a different girl on his arm. I didn't like him from the get-go, although I can certainly understand why so many of the girls did. He was charming. Handsome. Muscular."

Alex made a mental note to start lifting weights. "Did he hang around any of the islanders?"

Marcy puffed out her cheeks. "Not that I know of. He was usually tied up with a tourist girl. One from a rich family."

"Shoot. And I guess the last time you saw him was the end of the summer?"

"I can't give you an exact date," Marcy said, her voice slightly sarcastic. "But I guess he disappeared around the same time all of those seasonal workers did. As you know, one minute, the island is packed to the gills. The next minute, it's just a few of us. Happens every year."

After Alex finished his beer, he paid and tipped Marcy and headed up to the Pontiac Trail Head. Cindy had texted to say she was at their family house, having a glass of wine with their father. "Why don't you come up?" It was a good idea, especially because Alex wanted to thank his dad for his help with contacting Hank. Plus, he often felt aimless if he didn't see his father throughout the week. He was Alex's anchor.

Alex's childhood home was warm and comforting. Like always, he let himself in through the front door, which required no key. He could hear the soft tones of his father and sister chatting in the kitchen, where he soon found them with a bottle of wine. Brad, Elise's son who'd spent the winter on Mackinac, was seated at the island, reading the newspaper, and Diesel, his father's dog, was splayed across the rug.

"Alex!" Dean smiled. "Cindy said you might make the trek up here. How are you doing?"

Alex hugged his father and his sister and waved hello to Brad. Cindy poured him a glass of wine and explained she'd just come from Tracey and Emma's, where she and Megan had cooked the girls some chicken enchiladas.

"So, Megan's here for the rest of the semester?" Alex asked.

"I don't think so. Just until the baby comes," Cindy explained. "I'm so glad she's decided to stick around, though. That first semester without her was a doozy!"

"I think it's been healthy for both of you. Megan has been allowed to see who she is off the island, and you've been able to focus on your new life with Ron." Dean sipped his wine and gave Cindy an assuring nod.

"I hate when he's right," Cindy joked to Alex.

"Dad, thanks again for getting me Hank's number," Alex offered.

"Of course. How is his job down in Mississippi?"

Alex hadn't asked. "He said it's going well."

"Was he able to help you with your situation?" Dean asked.

"Unfortunately not." Alex sipped his wine and sighed.

"What's going on, little brother?"

"I finally figured out what's going on with Lily," Alex

explained. "And it's a doozy." He went on to explain the outline of Lily's dilemma. "Every lead so far has been a dead-end. I hate to go back to the Willow tonight and tell Lily I haven't made any headway."

"But you've only been at this one day," Cindy reminded him.

Alex palmed the back of his neck and tried to shove away thoughts of his own failure.

Dean crossed his arms over his chest and regarded Alex. Alex was suddenly frightened he would reprimand him. Instead, Dean said, "I'm proud of you for working so tirelessly to find this woman's husband and brother. What a selfless act."

Alex's cheeks burned.

"This is clearly one of the hardest times in Lily's life," Dean continued. "She came all this way with two young children on only a wish and a prayer. Despite that, she stumbled into you and discovered a true friend."

"And maybe a little more than friendship?" Cindy asked, wagging her eyebrows.

"It doesn't matter," Alex said, although his heart filled with the promise of it. "I just want to help her find peace. It's been such a lonely year for her. She doesn't deserve that."

"No. She doesn't." Dean eyed Alex curiously, as though he saw something in him he'd never seen before. "I'd love to meet her."

"Soon," Cindy said. "She's really lovely. I babysat her children during their first date."

"Cindy," Alex warned.

But Dean's face opened up with happiness. "You must bring her and the children over. I insist."

Alex couldn't remember a single time he'd brought a girl home. He sipped his wine and closed his eyes. His mind was fuzzy from adrenaline. For the first time in a very long time, he felt worthy of the Swartz family. He felt he finally belonged.

Chapter Thirteen

The next morning as Alex scrambled Lily's eggs, he got a call from Hank in Mississippi.

"Hello?" Alex was shocked to hear from him but tried to hide it from his voice. Hank had made it very clear the day before that he wanted nothing to do with Alex.

"Hi, Alex." Hank sounded resigned. "I was thinking about your little situation yesterday. I hate to say it, but something clicked about the fellow you're looking for."

"That's fantastic news. Anything helps."

"I'm decently sure he hung around with that Jasper guy. The one who lives in the cabin on the other side of the island? I'm sure you know him. He was normally in charge of the parties on the beach, right?"

Alex scribbled Jasper's name across a pad of paper. "That name rings a bell."

"But you didn't hear it from me," Hank countered. "I want to come back to Mackinac next summer. I don't need to have enemies when I get there."

"You have my word."

Alex dropped his phone and got back to the eggs just in the nick of time. Soon, he spread them across a yellow plate, crowded the eggs with bacon, and added a heaping pile of roasted potatoes. When he wheeled the breakfast tray to the elevator and then to Lily's door, she answered it and said, "You're too good to us." She then cleared the distance between them in the doorway and kissed him on the lips. A jolt of electricity bounced up and down Alex's spine.

In the suite, Kevin buzzed around with a plastic dinosaur toy while Ralphie rubbed the sleep from his eyes.

"We had a tough night," Lily explained as they set up the table by the window. "Ralphie woke up at two, then at four, then again at six-thirty."

"Poor guy," Alex said, rubbing the top of Ralphie's head.

"Suffice it to say, we're exhausted." Lily smiled. "But I have an appointment with Emma a little bit later today. Could you watch the boys while I go?"

"Of course!" Alex was thrilled to help. "We won't get into too much trouble. I promise."

That morning, Lily headed for Emma's, leaving Alex, Kevin, and Ralphie in a heap of toys and coloring books. At noon, she returned with burgers and French fries, and the four of them sat by the sitting room fire and ate. "It shouldn't be long now," Lily said of Emma.

"Are you nervous?" Alex asked.

"A little bit. I've done so many deliveries, but each one is different. I want to be sharp and ready for whatever happens," Lily explained. "Emma's afraid. I can feel it. But more than that, she's ready for this bedrest to be over."

After lunch, Alex cleaned up, kissed Lily, and headed out. He hadn't yet told her about his lead with Jasper, "the guy in the cabin," as he didn't want to get her hopes up. There was no reason Jasper knew anything; more than that, there was no reason Jasper should tell him anything. To Jasper, Alex was probably a yuppie, the son of the richest guy on the island. Why should he trust him?

In the Pink Pony, Marcy knew exactly which cabin Hank meant. She used the map on Alex's phone to drop a pin, then said, "Head here. As far as I know, Jasper hardly leaves his cabin during the winter. He's like a hermit until it hits fifty degrees."

Alex thanked Marcy, then headed up to Tracey's to borrow her snowmobile. His was still broken from the winter before. Tracey agreed, passing the keys through the front door with a smile.

"You hate riding snowmobiles," she teased.

"I hate walking four miles in the cold even more," Alex admitted.

"Where are you going? Is it a lead on Lily's brother?"

"Cindy already told you everything?"

"What kind of sister would she be if she hadn't?" Tracey waved Alex away. "Go on, Sherlock Holmes. Promise you'll tell me everything when you get back. And be careful on that machine! I know you're not the best rider."

Alex blushed and waved goodbye. Tracey kept her snowmobile in the little garage next to the garden. He unlocked it to find the shining machine within, primed and ready for a whip around the island. Alex told himself to be brave. After he eased the snowmobile into a clearing, he laced his leg over, adjusted the helmet over his head, and started the engine. It was just like riding a bike, he thought. Except that bikes were actually fun and not terrifying.

Alex took the snowy snowmobile trail along the beach, surprising himself with how fast he dared to go. In his thick coat, his gloves, and his thick wool socks, he felt impenetrable. He could have gone all afternoon.

Now that he was in his mid-forties, was he finally ready for a bit of thrill in his life? Why had it taken him so long?

He half-considered telling Lily later that he'd braved a snowmobile for her, but soon thought better of it. He didn't want to hint he was frightened of anything. He had to be continually strong for her and the boys.

Just as Marcy and Hank had said, Jasper's little cottage was located not far from Party Beach. Alex could just barely make out the outline of the cottage tucked between the snow-lined trees. When he couldn't ride any longer, he parked the snow-mobile, removed his helmet, and struck out through the forest. His heart banged powerfully in his chest. *Was Jasper one of those people who shot anyone who entered his property?* It was possible. Anything was.

When Alex reached Jasper's front porch, he set his jaw and knocked. Inside, a television roared. No answer. He knocked again, fear growing in his gut. Finally, the television quieted. Someone stomped across the hardwood, making the entire cabin shake. Then, a burly bearded man opened the door and towered over Alex.

"Hi." Alex hated the sound of his voice. "Are you Jasper?"

"Who's asking?"

Alex lifted his chin. "My name is Alex. A friend is missing. I have reason to believe you might know who he is."

Jasper cocked his eyebrow. He assessed Alex, his thick winter coat, and his parked snowmobile below. "You're the Swartz boy, aren't you?"

"I am. But I don't want any trouble. I'm just here looking for my friend. We're worried about him."

Jasper paused for another moment, then stepped back and opened the door wider. Alex thanked him and stepped inside. Dead animal heads lined the walls, a deer, a bear, and maybe an elk. On the table sat a bowl of apples. Alex wondered if Jasper did his own grocery shopping or if he called someone to deliver it so he could be a full-time hermit.

"Who's your friend?" Jasper closed the door and remained standing.

Alex fumbled his words. He explained what he knew about Lily's brother and that he and Jasper had worked at Arnold Line last year. At the mention of Lily's brother's name, Jasper stiffened.

"Are you sure you know what you're getting yourself involved with?" Jasper asked.

"Excuse me?"

Jasper took an apple and began to peel the skin with a paring knife. "That guy is a piece of work. I liked him at first. Really did. But I guess that's his secret. He lures people in and then tries to use them."

Alex got on his phone and brought up a picture of Lily's brother. "Are you sure we're talking about the same guy?"

Jasper eyed the photograph and nodded. "That's him, all right."

"I know he wasn't very nice to women."

"That was the least of it," Jasper muttered.

"Can you tell me a little bit more?"

Jasper's paring knife had reached the other side of the apple without breaking the skin. "I'm not usually one to tattle on guys like him."

"Whatever he's done, I won't get him into any real trouble," Alex said, although he wasn't sure he believed himself.

Jasper sighed. "You know how it gets around here in the summertime. Tourists come from far and wide to have the best weeks and months of their lives. Men like your friend understand that. And they come to profit off of that good time, if you know what I mean."

Alex shook his head. "I think you're going to have to be a bit more explicit."

"Drugs, Swartz. Your friend was a drug dealer. And he was a good one, from what I could tell. He operated all over the island, from the ferry docks to the bed and breakfasts to the parties on the beach. He couldn't be stopped. And sometimes, he asked the women he was involved with to help him. He thought he was unstoppable."

Alex's tongue tasted like cotton. This was not what he'd expected. "Are you sure?"

Jasper just laughed. Alex felt stupid.

"As far as I can tell, he left the island in August," Alex continued. "Do you have any idea of where he went? And was he traveling with someone?"

Jasper shrugged. "I made it clear to him I didn't want anything to do with his little business by the end of July. He wanted to drag me off somewhere. Alabama? Mississippi? Somewhere warm. Anyway, he was convinced he could triple his business down there over the winter months. Probably, he was right."

Alex's eyes widened. The puzzle pieces had begun to click into place. Still, it wouldn't be easy to deliver this news to Lily.

"Thank you for your time," Alex said soon after, watching as the rest of Jasper's apple peel fell to the ground. "Really. You've been a big help."

"Don't get too close to that guy." Jasper pointed the paring knife at Alex ominously. "He doesn't have your best interests at heart. He's in it for the money. That's it."

"I'll keep that in mind."

* * *

Alex returned Tracey's snowmobile and put the keys in the mailbox, as instructed. He then walked slowly back to the Willow Bed and Breakfast, his heart thudding with apprehension. Under his breath, he practiced his speech. *"Lily, there might be something about your brother you don't know." "Lily, your brother could be dangerous." "Lily, I don't know how to tell you this."*

When Alex entered the Willow, both Kevin and Ralphie bolted toward him and threw their arms around his legs. He teetered and nearly stumbled back, overwhelmed with the powerful wave of their love.

Lily jumped from the couch to save him. "Oh no! Did you take him prisoner?" Kevin and Ralphie collapsed on the carpet and giggled. Lily took Alex's hand in hers and kissed his cheek. She winced. "You're cold, Mr. Swartz. I think we'd better make you some hot chocolate. What do you say?"

In the kitchen of the bed and breakfast, Ralphie and Kevin sat at a little kid's table with coloring books as Lily boiled milk for proper hot chocolate. Alex rubbed his palms together. He couldn't tell Lily what he'd learned until the boys went to sleep. Until then, he had no idea what he would say. Perhaps he was boring. Perhaps his mind was a blank slate.

But with two young children, silence is not a longstanding problem. Kevin leaped up to show Alex his new art piece, which led to Ralphie doing the same. Soon, Alex sat at the kid's table as well, scribbling the hat of a cartoon character with a red crayon.

"You're a natural Van Gogh," Lily said as she placed the hot cocoa in front of him. "Should we reserve a gallery space for you?"

"Ha." Alex locked eyes with her and smiled.

When the boys were fast asleep, Lily joined Alex on the sofa in front of the fireplace with some empty glasses. They poured themselves some wine and collapsed in one another's arms, watching the fire as it licked the edges of its stone enclosure. Alex's heart thudded. This was the moment. He had to take it. Oh, but it was so perfect. Anything he said now would ruin it.

"Lily?"

"Hmm?" She smiled up at him sweetly.

"I have to tell you something."

Lily twitched away from him. "Oh, okay. What is it?"

Alex sighed. "It's about your brother. I might have learned something."

Lily's eyes widened with fear.

"I tracked down an old coworker of his from last summer. He lives on the other side of the island in a little cabin. When I told him your brother's name and showed him a photograph, he told me..." Alex shook his head, unsure of how to proceed. "He told me your brother is dangerous."

Lily's eyes narrowed. "That's ridiculous."

"I know. It must sound ridiculous to you." Alex palmed the back of his neck.

"I mean, you don't know my brother," Lily countered.

"I don't."

"And neither does this guy in the cabin. Not the way I do," Lily continued.

"Of course." Alex stuttered.

"I mean, why would he be dangerous? I've never heard anything more insane in my life."

"According to this guy in the cabin, your brother came to the island to deal drugs to tourists."

Lily's jaw dropped. "Drugs?"

Alex was in over his head. He'd just served the woman he wanted to love some very difficult information. Now, she looked very ready to shoot the messenger, so to speak.

On the coffee table, Lily's phone buzzed. Relief flooded Alex. Lily leaned forward to answer it. Her face focused, she said, "Hi, Tracey." A pause. Her eyes flashed. "All right. Don't panic. I'm on my way."

Chapter Fourteen

Emma had never experienced this type of intense pain in her life. Sweat dripped down her forehead; her t-shirt was drenched. The contractions had begun about two hours ago, and they were consistent at this point, so much so that Lily had joked, "The baby is suddenly just as impatient as you've been the past few weeks. He or she is ready to get out here and join the world."

Between contractions, Megan, Tracey, and Lily did their best to make Emma comfortable. They gave her ice chips, wiped cold clothes across her forehead, and tried to keep her entertained with light conversation; Megan reported news of their favorite celebrities and occasionally played their favorite songs, bumping around the room as Emma bobbed her head and smiled. When the next contraction poured over her, the room around her dimmed, and a strange, animal roar came from her throat. She felt entirely unlike herself. Worse, in only a few hours, she would be a mother. Could she actually handle it? Who did she think she was?

When Lily and Tracey were both out of the room after a

particularly heinous contraction, Megan perched at the edge of Emma's bed and tidied Emma's hair.

"I bet I look pretty crazy," Emma joked.

"You look gorgeous, Mama," Megan said.

"Now, you're just lying. I can't believe most women give birth with the men they love in the room. Can you imagine if Grant was here? He would be like, 'Babe, this is gross. Meet me at the bar later.'"

"Oh my gosh." Megan shivered with laughter. "I think you're better off without him."

"That's what everyone says," Emma returned. "I just hope you're all right."

"How are you doing in here?" Lily returned to the bedroom with a smile. "I've just been preparing the bathroom for delivery. As soon as it's time, we'll walk there together. How does that sound?"

"Sounds great," Emma quipped and then laughed. "Really good. I can't wait."

Another contraction tore through her. It twisted at the base, ran up her back, then moved to the front of her belly. Around her, Tracey, Megan, and Lily disappeared again, only to reappear a few moments later. Emma gasped for breath. Lily dropped between Emma's legs to check how dilated she was. It wasn't time yet. Emma groaned.

Megan turned the music back on and squeezed Emma's hand. Tracey returned with another bottle of water, and Emma drank, her eyes closed as her heartbeat pounded in her ears.

"I just don't know if I can," Emma heard herself cry. Her body erupted with tears that she hadn't expected. Tracey hurried forward to take the bottle of water before she spilled it.

"Honey! You can!" Tracey pressed a towel over Haley's forehead and cooed. "You're doing so well already."

"Focus on your breathing," Megan said. "You're just anxious. Breathe with me. In. Out. In. Out."

"Listen to your cousin and mother, Emma." Lily was reassuring, nodding at the far end of the bed. "They know you better than anyone. They know you'll get through this with flying colors."

Emma took a Kleenex and mopped herself up. Throughout, she eyed Lily, whose face was heavy with shadows. The clock on the wall read one in the morning, and she was ashamed for keeping everyone up all night.

"Lily? If you need to rest or something, you should." Emma surprised herself again with how normal she sounded after her outburst.

Lily shook her head. She looked mortified. "What? Oh. No, no. Emma." She stepped closer to her. "The only place in the world I want to be is here. I promised you I'd help you through this, didn't I?"

Emma nodded, furrowing her brow. "I'm sorry. I thought you seemed a bit off." She trailed off. She had the strangest intuition about Lily. Something was amiss.

Lily's eyes welled with tears. "I'm sorry to say I am. But I promise you, it's not affecting my work."

"Is this about your brother?" Tracey asked, clasping her hands together. "I can't imagine what it feels like not to know where a member of your family is. It must be devastating."

Lily sniffed and took a Kleenex from the box. "Alex met someone who says he knows him today."

"That's incredible," Tracey said. "Alex cares for you deeply. I knew he would crack the case."

Lily shook her head ever-so-slightly. "He doesn't know where he is. Only that he might have been involved in some pretty bad stuff here on the island."

Megan and Emma exchanged glances of pity.

"He was around all summer?" Megan asked.

Lily shrugged. "That's what he told me. Apparently, he worked at the Willow, at Arnold Line, and as a handyman. He must have known a hundred people. One of them must know where he is."

"And wherever he is, you think your ex-husband is there, too?" Tracey asked.

"That's the hope." Lily sighed. "It's not that I want him back. But he's the father of my children. They need him. Don't they?"

Emma groaned into the next contraction. Pain overwhelmed her. When it finished, she gasped into her hands, thinking again of her baby's father— a man her baby would never know.

When the contraction finished, and Lily had checked Emma again, Megan spoke.

"Emma and I were around all summer. Maybe we met your brother in passing. What's his name?"

"Grant. Grant Baxter." Lily sighed and dropped her gaze, as though saying the name overwhelmed her.

"What?" Megan and Emma howled in unison. Their eyes were buggy. Tracey leaped to her feet and began muttering to herself. "Oh my gosh. Oh my gosh. I can't believe this."

Lily shook her head. "Will someone please explain what's going on?"

Tears rolled down Emma's cheeks. She looked at Lily, really looked at her, and began to notice small features she shared with Grant. Why hadn't she noticed them before?

"Grant Baxter is the father of my baby," Emma whispered.

Lily looked at her, clearly shocked and confused. For a very long time, no one in Emma's room spoke. The tension was thick. But then, with a wild cry, Lily leaped toward Emma and wrapped her arms around her. The sound of sobbing echoed from wall to wall.

"Oh my god, Emma! You know what this means." Lily looked at Emma as tenderness engulfed her. "We're family."

Soon, Emma's contractions returned with a vengeance. All

memory of Grant was, for these moments, wiped clean. Lily returned to her professional midwife state and announced it was now time to move to the bathtub. The baby— her niece or nephew— would be born shortly.

"God bless us all," she whispered as she assisted Emma from bed.

* * *

Hours later, Emma sat in bed on clean sheets and cradled her baby girl. The fresh light of the morning peeked through the windows of her bedroom, and exhaustion overwhelmed her. Still, she was captivated by her beautiful baby, who slept so soundly in her arms. *How was it possible that a silly summer fling could result in such beauty and joy?*

After the birth, Megan collapsed on the couch in the living room. When Emma was all setup, Tracey went to bed, as well. Only Lily remained awake, packing up her things. They hadn't spoken of Grant in a long time. Maybe it had all been a dream.

"How are you feeling?" Lily asked quietly.

"Like I just gave birth."

Lily nodded and smiled. "It'll be like that for a while. I'll be back this afternoon to check on you. But you did so great, you know that? Both of you did." She gazed at the baby for a long time. Emma wondered if Lily saw something of Grant in the baby's face. To Emma, the baby looked like Tracey most of all.

"Can I ask you a question?" Lily asked.

Emma nodded.

"Why didn't you want Grant to know about the baby?"

Emma swallowed. It was a question she'd asked herself over and over again. "Truthfully?"

"Yes."

"I didn't think he'd care," Emma breathed.

Lily's face crumpled. After a long silence, she asked, "Do you think my brother was dealing drugs here on the island?"

Emma sighed. On the one hand, she'd never seen Grant deal drugs. On the other, he had always been evasive about where he was going and what he was up to.

"I really liked your brother," Emma said. "I crushed on him hard all summer long. I never saw him do anything illegal. Then again, I never saw him as much as I wanted to. I had this feeling he lived a whole other life, one he didn't want me to know. At the time, I assumed he was just seeing other girls. I'm sure that was true, too. But drugs?" Emma shook her head. "It's possible. But I don't want to believe it, either."

Lily's eyes glittered with sorrow. "I'm sorry my brother treated you so terribly. He doesn't have a great track record with women."

"I learned my lesson. No more handsome men who are too good to be true." Emma tried to smile, but she was too exhausted.

"Do you know anyone who might know where he's gone?" Lily asked.

Emma bit the inside of her cheek. In her mind, she scanned the wide variety of friends he'd had— nameless faces that had popped up spontaneously over the summer. "I might have an idea."

Chapter Fifteen

Alex had had quite a night. Paranoid that the children slept alone upstairs, he'd crept into Lily's room and slept next to Kevin, praying both boys would sleep till morning. He hadn't been so lucky. Ralphie had awoken at two-thirty and screamed to high heaven for his mother. This had alerted Kevin of the problem at hand, and over the span of the next hours, the brothers had worked themselves into a tizzy, genuinely terrified they would never see their mother again.

Now, it was seven in the morning. The boys were wired, and Alex bundled them up in their winter coats and hats and guided them around the bed and breakfast to the frigid sandy beach below. Ice crackled at the very edge of the lake, just above the sand, and the boys smashed it with their boots, delighting in destruction. Alex cracked several ponds, as well. Above, a beautiful winter day stretched across the sky, and sunlight poured through the naked trees.

Eventually, Kevin and Ralphie found sticks they liked— something most boys did— and proceeded to whack everything in their path. They snapped them over the sand, traced them in the water, and hit the trees along the beach. Alex laughed and joined them, smashing his stick against a very large stone. The stone had sat outside the Willow Bed and Breakfast for as long as he could remember. *Who had put it there? Had it been a part of someone's artistic vision for the beach?* He whacked it again, remembering that he'd done this very thing as a little boy. As the cancer had left his body and he'd regained strength, he'd been mesmerized by what his body was capable of doing.

That was the thing about growing up. You had to test your own boundaries. You had to push yourself to learn how to survive.

"Hey! What are you three doing down here?" Lily appeared on the beach in her beautiful winter coat. The boys immediately rushed her and collapsed in her arms.

"Mommy! Mommy!" It echoed down the beach.

Slightly embarrassed but too tired to care, Alex dropped his stick and joined the boys. Lily looked just as exhausted as he felt, but there was a glimmer in her eyes, a sense of hope.

"How's Emma?" Alex asked.

"She and the baby are healthy and happy," Lily breathed. "She was a trooper."

"I knew she would be."

Lily tucked a curl behind her ear. Before she could speak, Alex said, "The boys had trouble sleeping."

"I can see that."

"I think we'll have some very tired toddlers on our hands in no time flat." Alex adjusted Kevin's hat over his ears.

"Why don't we go inside and have some breakfast?" Lily suggested. The boys cried with excitement, collecting their mother's hands in theirs and waddling beside her to the back door. Alex brought up the rear.

Back in the kitchen, Lily began to brew a pot of coffee and poured the boys glasses of orange juice. The boys were red-cheeked and chatty, bouncing up and down in their plastic chairs. Alex placed a hand on Lily's back and kissed her on the cheek, his heart surging with love.

"You're such a remarkable woman," he whispered, then kissed her ear.

Lily turned into him and wrapped her arms around him. Into his chest, she whispered, "I'm sorry I acted so crazy when you told me what you'd learned about my brother."

Alex cradled her head. "It's okay. We don't even know if it's true."

Lily bristled and stepped back, glancing at her sons to make sure they were preoccupied. "I hate to say it, but I'm pretty sure it's true."

"Why do you say that?"

"He has a history of drug use," Lily said, her eyes returning to the coffee as it dripped into the pot. "He got clean a few years ago. At least, that's what I thought."

"But he was never a dealer?"

Lily shrugged. "He's good at hiding things from me. I mean, that's obvious, isn't it? I haven't been able to track him down for months."

For breakfast, Lily made them biscuits with sausage gravy. The boys ate until their pink eyelids began to drift to their cheeks.

"I think we'd better get them upstairs," Lily said.

"Sounds good." Alex collected Kevin in his arms, watching as Lily did the same with Ralphie. Together, they carried the slumbering boys to the suite, where they tucked them beneath their blankets. "They look so perfect right now. Don't they?" Alex asked.

Lily nodded. Her eyes filled with tears. Alex assumed she was overwhelmed from the drama of a full night of labor and delivery. Slowly, he guided her back downstairs, where he tossed more logs on the fire and wrapped his arms around her. She shook against him for a little while until she calmed.

"I don't know how to tell you this." Lily sniffed and swept a tear from her eye.

Alex kissed her shoulder. "You can tell me anything." This wasn't true, he thought immediately after. He didn't want to know if she still loved her ex-husband. He didn't want to know if she didn't see this as a long-term thing.

"Emma and Megan asked me the name of my brother," Lily whispered. "And when I told them, Emma said Grant was the father of her baby."

This was insanity. Alex sputtered. "Emma knew Grant all this time?"

Lily nodded. "Apparently, she did." She eyed Alex curiously, but Alex understood the question without her needing to say it.

"I never saw them together," Alex said. "Emma keeps her romantic life very separate from her family life. I can't say I blame her."

Lily sighed. "I figured. Tracey said she had never even met him. And she and Emma are thick as thieves."

"But does this mean Emma might know where Grant ended up?" Alex asked.

"She might know someone who knows." Lily shrugged. "She just gave birth, so I can't bother her with questions. Besides, Grant is a complicated figure in Emma's life. I don't get the sense he was very nice to her. He certainly wasn't around enough to learn she was pregnant."

"But she understands how important this is to you. And now that you're involved, she might want to tell Grant about his baby, after all." Alex wanted to be reassuring, although he felt out of his depth.

"Maybe." Lily sounded doubtful. Alex kissed her ear and her forehead.

Despite the coziness of the morning, Alex was now filled with a sense of dread. This Grant Baxter character had not only disappeared without a trace; he'd also been involved in drug dealing on the island, impregnated Alex's niece without any consequences for himself, and probably gotten the father of Kevin and Ralphie into an illegal situation. Grant was bad news. Alex wanted to tell Lily to forget about him, that Grant would contact her when he wanted to be found. Then again, he knew familial love didn't work like that. Lily would fight for the ones she loved most no matter what crimes they'd committed and no matter the mistakes they'd made. That was the sort of woman she was.

Again, Alex thought of his mother, dead only a few years now. Mandy would have adored Lily. He ached for Mandy's guidance, for her helping hand. Out here in a world without his mother, he so often felt aimless. He supposed everyone who'd lost their mothers did, in a way.

Chapter Sixteen

The first days of motherhood passed in a flurry of blissful moments, heart-wrenching terrors, painful breastfeeding sessions, adorable coos, and plenty of sleep. Emma felt in a haze, somewhere between this world and the next. Sometimes, Megan or Tracey appeared at her bedside to chat; other times, it was Lily. Emma took plenty of photographs of her sleeping baby, planning to dissect the first week of her baby's life when her brain worked properly again. As it was, she felt lost, afraid, and above all, overwhelmed with love.

It had taken Emma a full day to decide on her daughter's name. She had a list of five: Hannah, Fiona, Natalie, Oriana, and Jemma. To most, Megan and Tracy had turned up their noses. Emma laughed and called them snobs.

"Fiona Swartz," Emma said finally, her hand around Fiona's foot. "I think it's beautiful. A beautiful name for a beautiful baby."

On day four of Fiona's life, Emma got up the nerve to text a friend of Grant's, one she knew spent his winters in the nearby town of St. Ignace. It was miraculous she had his number at all. If she remembered correctly, she'd gotten it from Grant when Grant had known his phone was about to die. "We'll meet up later. Text Nathan's number." Incidentally, they hadn't actually met up that night, as Nathan had apparently lost his phone on a boat somewhere, and the two had floated off into the insanity of another reckless night.

EMMA: Hey, Nate! I don't know if you remember me. It's Emma Swartz from last summer. I worked at the fudge shop.

It didn't take long for Nathan to text back.

NATHAN: Woah, Em! Long time no see. How's it hanging?

Emma laughed, eyeing baby Fiona in her bassinet.

EMMA: Things have been crazy. I had a baby, if you can believe it.

NATHAN: What! Holy moly! Congratulations!

NATHAN: Uh. Wait. I'm not the father, am I? :)

Emma rolled her eyes.

EMMA: No. You're fine.

EMMA: But I might need your help with something.

EMMA: Could you come by my place? It's easier to explain face-to-face.

Nathan wrote back that he would be out of work by two that afternoon and could take the ferry as soon as possible. Emma was surprised and pleased that he'd jumped at the chance to help her. Then again, it's not like there was a whole lot to do in Northern Michigan in the dead of winter. What Emma had asked had intrigued him. Maybe that was enough.

* * *

That afternoon, Lily arrived at Emma and Tracey's place around one with a stack of pizzas and wide, manic eyes. Grateful for the use of her legs again, Emma opened the front door, hugged Lily close, and welcomed her into the fold. She was Fiona's aunt, after all. Megan was already on the couch with her laptop in her lap, and Tracey was in the kitchen, grabbing plates. It was the same constellation of people who'd helped Emma bring Fiona into the world, her circle of safety.

"How are you feeling?" Lily asked as she opened the pizza boxes along the coffee table.

"Not as tired today," Emma explained. "And grateful to use my legs again."

"Go easy on yourself," Lily said. "Give yourself time to heal. These are the easy weeks when Fiona will want to sleep the days away."

"Isn't she so precious?" Tracey filled her plate with pizza and collapsed on the couch. "Every time I hold her, I'm overwhelmed with how lucky I am. I'm a grandmother! When I was younger, I never even thought I would become a mother." Her eyes sparkled with memories.

"It's funny where life can take you," Lily agreed. "And goodness, I've started having baby dreams again. Fiona is such a darling! I can't believe my babies have already grown up so much. That time of my life is over."

Tracey and Emma exchanged glances. Both thought the same thing. If Alex had anything to say about it, Lily's baby-time was far from over. Emma had told her mother just the other night that she could imagine Uncle Alex with four babies plus two stepsons. "They'll fill up that house of his. Eventually, they'll need to move!" To this, Tracey laughed and said, "Gosh, I hope so. They should really take over Cindy's place. Her children are grown. It's Alex's time, now." Emma liked this thought. She liked thinking that Alex could have a future filled with the comforts of building a home.

Nathan arrived at three. On the stoop, he stomped the snow from his boots and rang the doorbell. Everyone in the living room froze, except for baby Fiona, who was asleep in Emma's arms and hadn't heard it anyway. Tracey hurried to the door to open it and exclaim, "Hello! Welcome to our home." She sounded too excited.

Nathan thanked her and stepped into the living room. He carried a bouquet of purple flowers, and he smiled his handsome smile, one that reminded Emma of impossibly blissful summer days with Grant and his friends.

"Wow! Emma! Look what you made!" Nathan laughed and gestured with the bouquet of flowers.

Emma blushed. "Are those for me?"

"They are." Nathan seemed proud of himself. If Emma had to guess, he hadn't purchased many flowers in his life.

"Sit down," Emma urged. "Would you like a piece of pizza?"

Nathan eyed the room-temperature slices hungrily. "Maybe just one. If it's not too much trouble."

"Not at all." Tracey disappeared and returned with a plate. "Fill it up with as much as you like."

Nathan did as he was told, acting more like a teenage boy than a man in his late twenties. When he sat, he chewed and swallowed a little too quickly. Emma hoped he wouldn't choke.

"So, Nathan." Emma glanced at Lily, trying to build her own strength. "Thanks for coming here. When I thought about people who could help us, I thought of you first."

Nathan again looked proud. "I'll do what I can." He took another bite.

"As you can see, I had a baby. But the baby's father is nowhere to be found. In fact, I've spent months trying to track him down, as I don't think it's right for a father not to know about his child."

Nathan nodded. "That makes sense."

Emma leaned forward, preparing to drop the bomb. "So. Do you know where he is?"

Nathan furrowed his brow, incredulous.

Finally, Emma added, "Grant Baxter, I mean."

Nathan's nostrils flared. "Grant is your baby's father?"

Emma nodded. She wanted to scream that Grant was the only man she'd dated the entire last year, but she kept that to herself. "He is. I'm one hundred percent certain."

Nathan dropped his chin to his chest. "Man. That guy. He's such a piece of work."

Lily's breathing had escalated. Emma glanced at her to find her panicked, sweat beading along her upper lip. Tracey, who sat next to her, rubbed her upper back, trying to calm her. Nathan hadn't noticed.

"Why do you say that?" Emma asked.

Nathan bristled. He dragged the back of his hand over his beard.

"Nathan, I really need to find him." She tilted her head toward baby Fiona, who was none the wiser. "It's bigger than any silly mistakes any of us made last summer. There's a baby involved, now."

Nathan bit his lower lip. He looked like a child in trouble at school. "He tried to get me involved in some of his schemes. You know?"

"Schemes?" Emma knew to play dumb.

Nathan nodded. "But I have a teenage brother, you know? So, when Grant started talking about dealing drugs here on the island, I said, 'This doesn't hurt rich people. This hurts people like my brother. Teenagers, whose brains aren't developed enough to understand the consequences.' He said he didn't care about the consequences. He was tired of being treated like a second-class citizen. He wanted money. Lots and lots of money. And he didn't care who stood in his way."

Lily had begun to cry very quietly. She seemed careful not to make any sharp movements.

"So, Grant was selling drugs?" Emma feigned surprise.

"I think he had a little ring here on the island," Nathan affirmed. "But he wanted to take things to the next level. That's when he came to me a second time to ask me to join him."

"What did he say?" Emma asked.

"He said he wanted to go south. He knew some high rollers down there who could set him up big. He threw some numbers at me. I mean, he was talking about six-figure salaries. It was the kind of money that would have changed my life. Again, I told him my worry about the people drugs actually affect— the teenagers and the lower class. He told me that's why we had to go to Florida. I didn't know anyone down there. At least that way, he said, I wouldn't know anyone we hurt."

"Gosh." Emma shook her head, genuinely overwhelmed at Grant's capacity for evil. How could she have been so wrong about him?

Suddenly, Lily piped up. "Nathan?"

Nathan turned to look her in the eye. "Yes, ma'am."

"Thank you for telling us this story. I know it's very hard to hear and very hard to tell. But we and baby Fiona appreciate you."

"Thank you, ma'am. To be honest, I haven't told anyone this story. I wouldn't rat on Grant."

"I know that. You're a good friend." Lily leaned forward, her eyes suddenly hungry. "Listen. Sometimes, Grant hung around with another guy. He's a little bit older than Grant. Named Reggie." Lily lifted her phone to show a photograph of her ex-husband, one of him smiling with the Mackinac Bridge behind him. "Do you recognize him?"

Nathan took the phone and smiled for the first time in minutes. "Reg! My man!"

"You know him?" Lily gasped.

Nathan nodded excitedly. He handed back her phone and got out his own, so he could show off a stream of photographs from a blissful day on Nathan's father's sailboat. The photos had been taken back in June, "the hottest day of the early summer," when they'd spent hours drinking beer, eating barbecue, and chatting about life.

Only when Nathan looked back up from the photos did he realize Lily was crying. His smile fell off his face. "Oh, gosh. I'm sorry! Really."

Lily used her sleeve to mop up her tears. "It's okay. Really. I just need to find him. I need to find both of them."

Nathan sighed. "If I had to guess, I'd say they're both somewhere down in Florida, working for those high rollers."

"Do you know anyone else Grant might still keep in contact with? Obviously, he doesn't have the same phone number. But maybe he gave his new one out to one of your mutual friends?" Emma asked.

Nathan furrowed his brow, took another bite of pizza, and stewed in silence for a long time. It was clear he knew he was in deep over his head— that lives were at stake.

"I'll see what I can do," Nathan said, his eyes resolute. He nodded first at Emma, then at Lily, recognizing the powerful need in Lily's face. After that, he swallowed the last of his pizza, grabbed his coat, and fled the house as though it was on fire.

Emma, Tracey, Lily, and Megan sat in stunned silence. In Emma's arms, Fiona cooed in sleep. An entire continent away, Grant Baxter lived out his wildest drug-dealing fantasies, probably with Reggie by his side. It was an impossible story, yet one they had to take in stride. With each day, they inched closer to them. One of these days, they'd find the truth.

Chapter Seventeen

I t was Valentine's Day when Alex finally got up the nerve to ask. Like always, he and Lily sat by the fireplace at the Willow as the boys slept upstairs, sharing a bottle of wine as the day faded into night. As Lily placed her head on his shoulder and sighed into him, he said, "Why don't you and the boys move in with me for a while?"

Immediately, Lily's head jumped from Alex's shoulder. Her eyes drank him in as though she'd never seen him before.

"I'm not asking for a forever commitment," Alex added quickly. "I know you've been through a lot. You were frank with me the first time we kissed. You don't know how long you'll stay, especially when you find your brother."

Lily nodded ever-so-slightly.

"But then again, it's uncomfortable to live in a bed and breakfast this long. You and the boys need a home. And I have a huge, empty house that I hardly use. Come and spend some time there with me. We can cook dinners, bake cookies for the boys, and make fires in the fireplace. Just like here." Alex's heart thudded with fear. "I have two guest bedrooms. One for you and the other for the boys." He wanted to make it clear he had no expectations.

Suddenly, Lily sprung forward, wrapped her arms around him, and breathed into his ear. "I don't know how I got so lucky, Alex. Thank you. I don't know how I'll ever repay you."

The next morning, Alex took the ferry to the mainland, where he purchased a toy train set, a pack of Legos for ages three-and-up, a stack of children's books, spare sheets, towels, and finally, a wooden rocking horse. When he returned to the ferry, the dock worker inspected his items with a curious eye. By nightfall, Marcy would hear all the gossip about Alex's "strange ferry boat ride." Alex just knew it.

Then again, wasn't it nice to have a bit of gossip going around the island about him for a change?

Alex spent the afternoon vacuuming, mopping, and making his house "child friendly" based on tips he'd read on the internet. He even lined Kevin's bed with stuffed animals and prepared the corner for the toddler bed, which would be delivered by carriage later that day. The heaviness of his "father-like" responsibility made him forget every sorrow he'd had in his life. He had people to care for; he had a job to do.

Lily and the boys arrived at Alex's place not long before dinner. Already, a fire crackled in the fireplace, a television beeped and bopped with cartoons, and a stew bubbled in a very large pot that Alex had never used. Alex wore a pair of corduroy pants and a burgundy button-down and prayed he didn't look overdressed for something as silly as this. Then again, it wasn't silly to him in the slightest. It was one of the greatest events of his life.

"Wow!" Lily's face was filled with awe. "What a beautiful place, Alex." She carried Ralphie into the living room. Kevin raced up beside her to stare, mesmerized, at the television. "Uh oh, Kev. Looks like Alex has some awesome cartoons on for you." She turned and winked at Alex, adding, "It's been hard not to have a TV around! Back at home, I sometimes plop them in front of it so I can get things done. Here in Mackinac, we've had to be much more creative in keeping them preoccupied."

"It's been a pleasure to hang out with them," Alex said.

Lily made sure Ralphie was set up, then closed the distance between herself and Alex to kiss him delicately on the lips. The impact was so startling and alive. Alex opened his eyes again with surprise and wrapped his hands around her waist. "Want a glass of wine?"

"I thought you'd never ask."

That night, Alex was at peace. He prepared the stew, buttered Ralphie's bread, re-filled Lily's wine, and even helped with bath and reading time. From the doorway, he watched Lily tuck Kevin into bed and snap off the lights. His chest brimmed with love.

Back downstairs, Lily and Alex put another log on the fire, poured additional glasses of wine, and watched snow flutter past the window. Alex told her the Willow would be closed for cleaning and refurbishing until summertime, and Lily laughed and asked, "Were you just keeping it open for us?" Alex grimaced, embarrassed, but eventually confessed it was true. "But if you hadn't said yes to moving here, you could have stayed at the Willow forever."

Lily tilted her head. Her lips were stained plum from the wine. After a long and easy silence, she asked him, "You were never married. Right?"

Alex's throat tightened. This was not easy territory. "No. I wasn't."

Lily gestured around the big room with its vaulted ceilings. "Why do you have this house?"

Alex forced himself to look her directly in the eye. "Because. I always visualized myself having a family. I threw myself into work and helped my father's business boom. After that, I bought a big house. I thought I was ticking off the necessary boxes to build a perfect life. But unfortunately, the wife never came. The rooms were never filled."

Lily's eyes caught the firelight. "You deserved it."

Alex bristled. "I've always been difficult to know. Any date I went on wasn't exactly enjoyable for either party. I always found a reason not to like my date after a drink or two. She probably found a reason not to like me from the get-go."

"That's silly, Alex. What's there not to like about you?"

Alex couldn't help but laugh. But Lily's face tightened.

"Listen to me very carefully," Lily breathed. She wrapped a hand around Alex's upper bicep, and the touch was intoxicating. "You're a remarkable man. You are so deserving of love and family. Don't let your brain tell you anything different. Okay?"

"Okay."

"You promise me?"

Alex didn't have a choice. "I promise."

Lily settled back against him and studied the fire. "I know what it's like to have your brain go haywire on you. But you have to stand your ground. You have to fight it. You have to remind yourself every day of your worth."

Alex hadn't expected such a volatile response. His heart widened to carry the depths of his love for her. That night, as she slept in the room on the other side of his wall, he stared into the darkness over his bed and tried to remind himself of his own worth, just as she'd told him to do. It almost worked.

* * *

The phone call that changed everything came the next afternoon. Lily answered it with a bright hello, but her tone darkened immediately after. "I can be there in an hour." Lily set the phone on the counter in Alex's kitchen. Suds from washing dishes hung on Alex's wrists.

"That was Emma. Apparently, Nathan has learned something about Reggie and Grant. She wants to tell me in person." Fear made her eyes glisten.

Alex cut the water and wrapped his arms around her, careful not to cover her with soap. She allowed a single sob to escape, but then quieted.

"It's stupid. I don't know anything yet," she muttered as she tidied up the kitchen. "I have to keep it together."

Alex and Lily were quiet as they prepared the boys for the trip to Emma's. Ralphie seemed uninterested in his snowsuit and ran through the kitchen and dining room until Alex could apprehend him in the living room again. He howled and laughed, thinking it was all a game.

On the walk, Alex pushed Ralphie and Kevin in a wheel-barrow. Together, he and Lily waved at other walkers, most of whom eyed Alex, then Lily, then the children with heavy curiosity. The children had a hoot in the wheelbarrow, waving at everyone. Their mittens shook.

"Bunch of gossips," Alex muttered under his breath.

"Gossip makes the world go round," Lily said. "I get it."

At Emma and Tracey's, Alex parked the wheelbarrow out front and lifted Ralphie while Lily helped Kevin onto the walk-way. Kevin knew by now to scamper up the steps and ring the doorbell. He even knew to greet Tracey by name.

"Hello, boys." Tracey smiled sadly at Kevin and Ralphie, then lifted her head to greet Alex and Lily. "I'll watch them in the back. Emma's in the living room, waiting for you."

Lily thanked her. In the foyer, Alex and Lily removed their coats and watched as Ralphie and Kevin scampered after Tracey, who tempted them with treats and toys. Emma sat, puffy-eyed, on the couch in the living room with a folder in front of her on the coffee table.

"Hello." Emma stood, adjusting her sweatshirt over her frame.

Alex hugged his niece and asked about Fiona, who was

apparently already growing like a weed. Lily hugged Emma, which was probably a mistake, as she immediately burst into tears. Alex collected Lily in his arms and held her tightly until she quieted. The mood was dark.

"Thank you for coming over," Emma began. She gripped the folder on the coffee table. "As you know, I asked Nathan to do some digging about Grant and Reggie's whereabouts. He sent me a few articles this morning. I've printed them out." She closed her eyes then, as though she was unsure if she wanted to pass the folder over.

Alex had to be the one. With one arm wrapped around Lily, he took the folder with his free hand and flipped it open. There was the print-out. At the top were two striking images of two very serious-looking men. The man on the left was labeled as Grant Baxter, while the man on the right was Reggie Franklin.

The headline above the photographs read:

One Dead, One Injured in Crash. Found In Possession of One Hundred Thousand in Drugs.

A shiver raced through Lily's body. Alex reread the headline, thinking it could change. And then, he forced himself through the specifics of the early part of the article. Reggie Franklin had died immediately at the scene of the accident. His brother-in-law, Grant Baxter, had been taken into custody and was awaiting trial. For his crimes, he faced up to twenty years in prison.

This was the end of the road. This was what Lily had come all the way to Mackinac to find.

"It happened in October." Lily's voice was nearly impossible to hear. She pulled the article from Alex's fingers and read and reread the date. Her eyes filled with tears. "He's been dead four months. And I haven't even known."

Emma's eyes were stormy. "I'm so sorry, Lily. I hate to bring you this news. I really do."

Lily allowed the article to flutter to the ground. Somewhere in the back of the house, Ralphie and Kevin giggled madly together. They were two brothers who'd lost their father. Probably, they wouldn't even remember him.

"I should be angry at him," Lily whispered. "At both of them, really. But all I can think is— what a waste. What was it for? A bit of extra money? A good time?" Lily closed her eyes and shook her head. "My children didn't deserve this. I didn't deserve this. Emma, you, and Fiona didn't deserve this, either."

Emma's gaze dropped to the ground. Slowly, Lily reached across the couch and took Emma's hand.

"Thank you for your help, Emma. Without this information, I would have been swirling in purgatory for a whole lot longer. Maybe forever. With this news, maybe, just maybe, I can find peace."

Tears dripped from Emma's eyes. "I hope so."

Chapter Eighteen

Cindy agreed to take Ralphie and Kevin for the night. After a brief and very quiet walk, Megan greeted Alex and Lily at the front door of their beautiful home, squatted down to hug the little boys, and then lifted them up. She winced and tried to joke. "This is some real weightlifting, Lily. No wonder you're in such good shape."

Lily laughed kindly but couldn't seem to make her lips smile.

"Thanks for doing this," Alex said, waving into the living room, where Michael, Margot, Cindy, and Ron sat together.

"Call me if you need anything," Lily said.

Cindy hustled up to hug Lily goodbye. In her ear, Cindy whispered something Alex couldn't quite hear. Lily blinked back tears and said, "Thank you." Alex had to assume this was the secret language of mothers, of women lifting one another up through time.

Back at the Pontiac Trail Head, Lily stood and gazed out across the Straits of Mackinac. The orange light was astounding against the dark clouds that billowed along the water. Alex wrapped his arms around her and felt the steady thump of her heart. How strange it must have felt to go on living when the father of your children had passed on.

When the air was too sharp with a chill to stay still, Lily and Alex returned downtown, got burgers to go, and sat in Alex's living room in front of the fire. Lily nibbled at the end of a French fry but seemed uninterested in her cheeseburger. Alex sipped his beer and tried to think of one thing to tell her. One thing that would lessen the pain. There was nothing.

"He really was a very mean man," Lily said spontaneously and chewed up the rest of her French fry. "I know you shouldn't speak ill of the dead. But ever since I learned of his death, all I've thought about are the beautiful memories. I've thought about when we brought Kevin back from the hospital. About when we got back together after a separation and decided to have Ralphie. About the little quirks he had that made me laugh. About the silly jokes he told."

Lily shook her head. Her eyes were resolute. "But in all honesty, there were so many more bad times than good. He was cruel and manipulative. I was terrified the boys would take a page from his book. I had nightmares they would one day look at me the way Reggie had looked at me and call me one of those horrible names."

Alex placed his hand on her upper back.

"I loved him. For a long time, I did love him. I built a whole life with him, for goodness sake." Lily closed her eyes. "And I'm not glad he's dead. I wouldn't have wished that on him. In fact, I wanted more than anything for him to go to therapy. I wanted him to work on himself. I wanted him to become the man the boys and I needed him to be. Instead, he died in this horrific crash. And meanwhile, my brother faces twenty years in prison. It's all so pointless. All this pain. I can't figure out what it's for."

Alex pushed the burgers and fries to the side so that he could fully wrap his arms around her.

"Listen to me, Lily. You didn't deserve his abuse. You don't deserve anyone's abuse. You're a good person. A great mother."

Lily shivered in his arms.

"He was cruel to you. He had no right to be."

Lily had begun to cry. "I know. But I don't want to hate him. He died. And he shouldn't have died."

Alex's heart burst open. As they sat there together before the crackling fire, Lily's tears stained his shirt, and she howled into his chest until she was too exhausted to make a sound.

That night, she asked to sleep in Alex's bed, as she didn't want to be alone. For hours, Alex stared into the darkness and listened to her soft breathing. Sometime after four, he finally drifted off to sleep, only to rise at six, when she awoke to cry again. He didn't notice his own fatigue. In those hours, he lived only to comfort her.

The next morning, Alex and Lily sat downstairs in the kitchen and sipped coffee quietly. Lily's eyes were puffy, but her face was otherwise serene, capturing the bright light of the new day. New snow piled on the windowpanes and back porch. Alex made a comment about shoveling it aside, but remained in his pajamas, too exhausted.

Around noon, Cindy, Dean, Tracey, and Elise brought Ralphie and Kevin back to Alex's place. Lily knelt to greet her boys as they showed her the pictures they'd drawn and the little clay sculptures they'd made. Last night, Lily had asked Alex how she should tell her boys about their father's death. *What language was necessary for a three-year-old and a twenty-month-old?* They'd decided to research together over the next week. There were plenty of books on the subject. Apparently, unthinkable things like this happened all the time.

"We brought supplies to have a big pancake brunch." Elise smiled and squeezed Alex's elbow. "I hope you're hungry."

Dean removed his coat, hung it on the coat rack, and swallowed Alex in a bear hug. Alex was surprised at how comforting it felt to be held by his father. When the hug broke, Dean said, "I always knew you were a compassionate person, Alex. But what you've done the past few weeks is remarkable."

Alex shook his head. How could he explain that he couldn't have done anything else? His love for Lily made everything else natural, as easy as breathing.

"Remember to ask us for help when you need it," Dean continued. His eyes burned with the love he had for his family. "You are not in this alone. None of my children are. And when I'm not around..." He trailed off for a moment, looking misty-eyed. "I know you'll have each other. Forever."

Alex's throat tightened. Why did his father have to bring up his own demise on such a sunny morning? Alex tried to make a deal with himself not to get too upset.

In the kitchen, Elise stirred pancake batter in one of Alex's largely unused glass bowls. "You have so much cooking supplies, Alex." Elise sounded impressed. "Why don't you ever invite us over for dinner?"

Alex blushed and glanced at Lily. "I'll have to do that more often from now on."

"Oh! What will you cook?" Cindy brewed another pot of coffee and reached for more mugs in the cabinet.

"Alex is a fantastic cook," Lily added. "He served the boys and I beautiful meals at the Willow. For a little while, I thought he had someone else working in the kitchen. Someone professional. But it didn't take me long to figure out it was all him." Lily's eyes shone. "Especially when you started telling me about the important vitamins and nutrients in each piece of food, which you'd apparently researched specifically for Ralphie and Kevin."

Alex blushed and sat at the kitchen island. "I was so obvious, wasn't I?"

"No. You were adorable." Lily cupped his wrist with her hand. She then turned toward Cindy and asked, "How were the boys last night? I hope they didn't get into too much trouble."

"They were darlings," Cindy said. "But they ran Megan ragged. She insisted on sleeping in, but says she'll be here in a little while."

"Is she going to go back to Michigan State now that the baby is born?" Alex asked.

Cindy's lips fell into a line. "You know what? I don't know. The online classes seem to be working out just fine. Then again, I have a hunch she kind of likes her new life down in East Lansing. How dare she, right?"

"She always told me she plans to find her way back," Elise said.

"It's just like with Michael," Cindy admitted. "He was gone for three years, finding himself. When he got back, he was ready to be my Michael again."

Lily sighed at the cozy image of her boys in the living room, where they played with little toy trucks, making beeping noises as they backed up across the carpet. "I wonder what kind of chaos they'll put me through in twenty years."

"It's all a blessing," Cindy assured her quietly. "Even the most painful moments. Because you'll know your sons are living. They'll be testing their boundaries. They'll be trying to figure out what makes them happy."

"And in the end, I just want them to be happy," Lily whispered, close to tears again.

"That's what any good mother wants," Cindy assured her.

As they sat down for pancakes, Elise's son, Brad, arrived. He'd spent the winter at his Grandpa Dean's, just a few houses away from Elise and Wayne's new place. There, he'd attempted to pick up the pieces of his life, which had gone off-course in Los Angeles. As Alex was a small-town guy from a very tiny island, the thought of trying to make it in the big city genuinely terrified him. He hoped Brad would stick around Mackinac, if only to understand the magic of a quiet life.

"Hi, buddy!" Elise brimmed with happiness as he sat beside her.

Brad smiled his handsome, twenty-three-year-old smile and took a pile of pancakes, which he slathered with maple syrup. When he was finished with his construction, he raised his eyes to Lily's and said, "Lily, I want to tell you I'm very sorry for your loss." It was the first anyone had mentioned it all morning.

And for some reason, as it came from Brad— a very young man who had nothing to do with the situation— it felt honest and pure. Lily nodded and said, "Thank you. I'm just grateful to be surrounded by such a strong and loving family this morning. It reminds me of all the reasons I left Reggie in the first place." She paused and added, "I'll miss him forever. But I think that's just a part of life."

Everyone nodded for a moment, considering what she'd said.

"I still miss my ex-husband," Elise chimed in. "Don't get me wrong. I'm grateful we're not together. That part of my life came to a very necessary close. But sometimes, in the mornings, I think about how he took his coffee or the fact that he always needed help with the crossword."

"There are things I miss about Fred," Cindy breathed. "And goodness. I've spent more than twenty years missing my first love, Jeremy."

Tracey bowed her head, her eyes on her pancakes. "I met a man over the summer and fell in love much too quickly. He lives in Los Angeles; I live here. Our romance has no bearing in reality. But at night, I mourn the life we could have had. There was so much love there."

Dean was the last to speak. He clasped his hands together over the table and closed his eyes. "Mandy Swartz was the love of my life. In no way was I the perfect husband. But every day, she guided me. She helped me understand how to love and love well, which involves learning how to forgive yourself. Without her, I would have been a crummy father. I suppose it goes without saying that I miss her every single day. My dreams about her are gorgeous, though. Filled with sunlight. We're usually out on the water, talking about something inane, like going to the grocery store before heading home."

As Alex sat and listened to his family's stories, he imagined himself forty years from now, an old man. Would he be allowed to know someone enough to miss them this much? Would he be allowed such a capacity for love?

He ached for it. Now in his mid-forties, he knew it was the only way to a true and beautiful life.

Chapter Nineteen

It was incredible how much luggage a tiny baby of six weeks old needed. Despite sleeping most hours of every day and consuming nothing but breast milk, little Fiona required diaper bags, multiple outfits, blankets, cushions, wraps to hang from Emma's chest, her stroller, and so much more. Emma and Tracey packed for Fiona for over two hours before they scrambled to pack their own suitcases. In hers, Emma shoved several sundresses with loose-fitting bottoms, a one-piece swimsuit, sunglasses, and a few books (just in case Fiona let her read), along with snacks like granola bars, protein bars, Swedish fish, and string cheese.

Megan knocked on their front door at fifteen past two. "Hello! Is anyone in there?"

As Emma opened the door, immaculate April light shone through the glass and blinded her. "My gosh. It really is almost spring, isn't it?" The temperature hovered around forty-seven degrees, a marked difference from the fifteens and twenties of January and February.

"It's spring break, baby!" Megan laughed and wrapped her arms around Emma.

"Right. Your first college spring break," Emma said, stepping back to let Megan inside with her suitcase. "And you're spending it with a six-week-old baby."

"Not just any six-week-old baby," Megan corrected. "Fiona Swartz is known across Florida as a wild partier. Sometimes, she even stays up all night just because she feels like it."

"Only a few times." Emma winced.

"Hello, my favorite niece!" Tracey hustled into the living room to hug Megan close. "This dress is darling. You look ready for spring break! But you're going to freeze on the ferry."

Megan giggled. "My mom said the same thing. I told her spring break is more of a state of mind, and you have to dress the part."

Tracey didn't look convinced. She grabbed an extra scarf and a pair of snow pants for Megan and stuffed them into the top of her suitcase.

"Remember when the airlines lost your suitcase in Los Angeles?" Megan asked slyly.

Tracey huffed. "You're not referring to the nightmarish day when I ran into Emma's real father for the first time in over twenty years. Are you? If so, may I suggest we reserve this conversation for after I've ordered a glass of wine on the plane?"

"Mom gets nervous on planes," Emma reminded Megan.

Tracey pointed her finger accusatorially. "This reminds me. The last time we were on a plane together, you refused to get a glass of wine with me. You ordered Diet Coke!"

Emma rolled her eyes.

"You already knew you were pregnant! I can't believe how long you kept it from us." Tracey pretended to be hurt, then turned to lift Fiona from her bassinet. "She didn't want me to know about you. But I found out anyway. Didn't I, Fi?" In response, Fiona cooed.

"She's already manipulating her," Emma teased.

"It's what grandmothers are supposed to do," Megan said. "My mom has Michael's daughter wrapped around her finger."

Down at the ferry docks, Lily already waited for them. Her suitcase was planted firmly beside her, and her jaw was set, resolute. Quietly, she greeted them with hugs and said, "I can't believe it. We're really going."

A moment of silence passed.

"I'm surprised Alex and the boys aren't here to see you off," Tracey said.

"They were in the middle of an epic Lego construction. I didn't want to interrupt them," Lily explained. She then placed her hand on her heart as she said, "I've never been away from them this long."

Megan swung her arm over Lily's shoulder and said, "You know what that means?"

Lily shook her head.

"We're going to try to find a way to have a little bit of fun." Megan hesitated. "I know we're going to the Florida Keys for a very difficult reason. But there will be seafood there. Drinks. Sandy beaches. Gorgeous sunsets. We've been frozen solid in Michigan all winter long. It's time for us to thaw out. Don't you think?"

Just as Tracey had warned, Megan nearly froze on the ferry boat. She shivered on the bottom deck with a mug of coffee as, one after another, Lily, Emma, and Tracey hustled to the top deck to watch the island recede. Emma was careful to leave Fiona wrapped up on the bottom deck, safe from the severity of the winds. Up on top, Emma was mesmerized by how easily the island disappeared into the lake, as though the enormity of her life was really a speck.

Their flight was planned to take off from Detroit that

evening. They arrived two hours ahead of time, which allowed Emma to go through the barrage of baby chaos, ensuring that both she, Fiona, and all of Fiona's odds and ends made it to the Florida Keys. When they got through security, Tracey took Fiona for a little while so that Emma could use the bathroom, buy a bottle of water, and give herself a pep talk. No, most women wouldn't have traveled with a six-week-old baby. But both Lily and her pediatrician had cleared it, saying Fiona would probably sleep the entire way.

On the plane, Emma and Megan were seated in one row, with Lily and Tracey ahead of them. They ordered glasses of white wine as Fiona slept soundly, her angelic face very impressive to the flight attendants, who said she was "their best passenger of the day." Emma's glass of wine was on the house.

The Florida Keys rental house had been built like an Italian villa along a stretch of white, sandy beach. Elise's friend in the television business owned it, and she'd gotten them an incredible deal. Elise herself was off visiting Penny in Los Angeles and couldn't make it, but she'd sent along a gift basket of champagne, cheese, and chocolate, along with a note: "Wish I could be with you this week. All my love, E."

It was ten-thirty by the time they arrived. All five of them were starving. Emma scarfed a few snacks and breastfed Fiona, put her to sleep in the bassinet they'd rented for the house, then joined Tracey, Megan, and Lily on the gorgeous patio, where they'd begun to arrange the food they'd ordered from a fish restaurant down the block. Buttery cod, fried octopus, succulent salmon, roasted potatoes with spices, freshly baked rolls, bright green salads, and several types of white wine lined the table. Tracey lit a candle, and it cast long shadows along the table.

"This looks perfect," Emma breathed.

"I'm glad we ordered it on the taxi ride here," Tracey said with a laugh.

Megan tore open a dinner roll and smeared it with soft butter that sparkled with inlaid sea salt. "Even the butter is ridiculous."

Lily poured wine for everyone and lifted her glass. Silence fell over the table. "I want to thank you all for coming down here with me. This was a trip I knew I needed to take, but I don't know if I would have been brave enough to do it alone."

"We wouldn't have let you do this alone," Tracey said softly.

"This mess is partially my mess, too," Emma affirmed.

"It's just like Grandpa always says. We have to lift each other up," Megan said.

Together, they ate as Florida stars sparkled in the inky black sky above them. Twenty feet away, the ocean rushed over the sands and then receded back into the darkness, each wave curving closer with the tides.

"When are you meeting Grant?" Tracey asked.

Lily and Emma locked eyes. This had been a question of some debate, as the prosecutors and Grant's defense lawyers had changed the trial dates several times.

"They said tomorrow is out of the question," Lily explained.

"But the one after tomorrow," Emma affirmed.

Tracey eyed Emma curiously. "You sure you want to go through with this?"

Emma nodded. She'd considered it over and over and lost so many nights of sleep. Ultimately, before Grant went to prison for decades, she wanted him to know about his daughter. This was especially true now that Lily was a part of the equation. Already, Lily and Alex's love seemed a powerful anchor, one they wouldn't rip up too quickly. Lily would be Fiona's aunt in every single way. Grant deserved to know that.

"If I know my brother at all," Lily began hesitantly, "there is a part of him that will live for this. Telling him about Fiona is a tremendous gift. I can't thank you enough for doing it."

Emma nodded and sipped her wine. On top of everything, a very small part of her still loved that adorable and wildly fun man she'd met last summer. Maybe that version of Grant had never really existed. Maybe she'd just made him up in her mind.

Because it was the Florida Keys and because they had very little else to do, they spent the first full day in the sun. Emma was very careful to monitor Fiona's temperature levels, to keep her away from overexposure. But with Tracey, Megan, and Lily there to help, Emma was able to run headlong into the ocean with her arms out on either side. She was able to feast on more fish, drink a fruity cocktail, and let her hair dry into wild and salty curls. Her love for her baby seemed to make her love for the world and all its gifts even more powerful. When she saw a tourist litter, she wanted to scream at him for not respecting the planet. "Doesn't he know this world will belong to my daughter one day? We're supposed to keep it beautiful!"

That night, as Emma fed Fiona back at the villa, she accidentally eavesdropped on Tracey's conversation in the next room. A better person would have closed the door completely, but Emma's interest was piqued.

"It's been a dream, Malcolm. Really. My daughter looks happier than ever as a new mother. Lily is devastated after everything that happened, but she's been swimming and drinking cocktails with the rest of us. Oh, and Megan keeps joking it's our college spring break."

There was silence for a moment. Emma tried to imagine the other end of the line. Perhaps back in Los Angeles, the handsome movie director spoke with tenderness, grateful to be kept in Tracey's orbit. Perhaps he watched his deaf child and smiled at her as his heart ached to be near Tracey again. Perhaps one day, their love would find a way to flourish.

For not the first time, Emma wondered if she should let her mother go. Did she actually need Tracey to stay on Mackinac to help raise Fiona? Would Tracey resent her for holding her back?

Megan peeked her head into Emma's room. "Hey! Is she asleep?"

"Just about," Emma whispered.

Megan tip-toed into Emma's room and sat at the edge of the bed, watching as Emma placed Fiona lovingly into her bassinet.

"You're getting good at this mom stuff."

"It is not easy," Emma admitted. "I thought motherly instincts would take over immediately, but I felt like I had to learn everything."

"At least you only have to learn it once," Megan pointed out.

"I have a feeling that I have to keep learning as I go," Emma said. "As soon as I get the hang of one thing, she gets a little bit bigger, and things change again."

"She's always one step ahead of you." Megan laughed gently.

Out the window, a large and pregnant moon hovered over an island that seemed a part of another dimension. It seemed impossible that Mackinac still existed, a near-frozen rock thousands of miles north.

"This is not a normal college spring break. Is it?" Emma asked as she sat cross-legged on the bed next to her cousin. Between them were over twenty years of shared memories. She felt them stretched out behind them, impossibly beautiful yet lined with the tragedy and confusion of youth.

Megan chuckled. "I don't know what you mean."

Chapter Twenty

T he next morning, Lily and Emma took the rental car downtown, leaving Fiona, Tracey, and Megan at the villa. Both Lily and Emma wore dark dresses and sensible heels. Their makeup was simple yet perfect, eyeliner straight, and lipstick practical. On the drive, Emma held her knees and watched the traffic, remembering an article she'd read about tourists in rental cars and how often they got into accidents. Still, Lily was a good driver, and she parallel parked them directly next to the jailhouse, cut the engine, and said, "Well. I guess this is it."

Inside, Grant's defense lawyer greeted them with stiff handshakes. He was a balding man of about fifty-five, one of those lawyers who was given to criminals who had no other option. There was very little light left in his eyes, as though the legal system had chewed him and his clients up too much. He had no fight left.

"I'm Grant's sister," Lily said. "And this is Grant's very good friend, Emma."

The lawyer nodded. Emma had the sense he immediately

forgot their names, as they weren't pertinent to the case. He explained the day's events, including the trial, which was set to begin at four that afternoon. He then told Lily and Emma they had fifteen minutes to speak with Grant if they chose. He was being held a few rooms away and would probably be happy to see familiar faces, as he'd had "quite a trying few months." "He knows what he did was wrong. That doesn't necessarily make any of this any easier," the lawyer explained.

Emma squeezed Lily's hand. "You go first."

Lily nodded, her face stoic. "Do you want me to tell him you're here?"

Emma hesitated. This was a very good question, one that didn't have a correct answer. "You should focus on what you want to talk to him about. I'll take care of my part."

Lily followed a security guard down the hallway and left Emma and the lawyer alone in a waiting room filled with orange plastic chairs. A Bible quote hung in a frame on the wall. After a few minutes, the lawyer told Emma he had to make a few calls to other clients, and he stepped into the humid morning. Minutes later, Emma could hear him speaking rapid Spanish.

Megan texted a few minutes later.

MEGAN: Have you seen him yet?

EMMA: No. Lily went first. I'm next.

EMMA: Trying not to freak out.

In response, Megan sent a photo of Fiona asleep on Tracey's chest. Warmth spread through Emma's fingers, arms, and legs. It was remarkable what love did to you. It was an immediate balm.

After twenty minutes, the security guard returned to fetch Emma.

"Where's Lily?" Emma asked, surprised she hadn't come back first.

"She's on the other side. You'll see her when you finish," he explained.

This sounded ominous. Still, much like childbirth, Emma could do nothing but trust the process. She followed after the guard down that same long hallway. A lightbulb flickered overhead. *Who was responsible for changing it?*

The guard opened the second-to-last door on the right. "Grant Baxter. You have another visitor."

And then, that voice. Emma hadn't heard that voice since last summer. It was deep and intoxicating as nougat. In her memories, that voice whispered to her late at night, making up fantastical stories of a future wherein they got a little house on the beach and lived out their days in the sun. He'd made her feel like the only woman in the world.

It had all been a lie. Still, in her memory, the lies had felt so beautiful and true. Any woman like Emma would have fallen for them. Love was meant to be something you believed in, no matter what the cost.

Emma stepped into the doorway. On the other side of a wall of bars sat a desk that was nailed to the ground; behind that, sat Grant. This version of Grant was pale and stringy, his cheeks sunken from months in jail. His eyes were hollow, and his head had been shaved of his wild, boyish curls.

"Oh my God. Emma?" He was incredulous.

Emma was shaken to the core. Was this a mistake? She stepped into the room and sat in the chair across from him. Behind her, the guard closed the door and left them alone.

Grant's smile was still just as handsome as ever. It triggered something in Emma's heart, another memory of why she'd fallen for him.

"I can't believe you're here. Wow. Emma, you were always so loyal to me." He looked amazed. "Maybe, if I get out of here, we can try again. Really try this time."

Emma stiffened. *Loyalty?* She wasn't there for any loyalty

to him. She wanted nothing to do with him! "Actually, I'm here for another reason."

Grant's smile fell. "Go on."

Emma took a staggered breath. Was she strong enough for this? "Right around the time you disappeared last summer, I learned I was pregnant. I wasn't going to tell you. To be honest with you, I didn't think you deserved it."

Grant furrowed his eyebrows but remained very quiet.

"In January, a mysterious woman and two children came to the island. I came to find out that woman was a midwife. During the tail-end of my very difficult pregnancy, she was there for me. Imagine our surprise when that woman turned out to be your sister, who was on the island to look for you."

Grant's jaw dropped. Still, he was wordless.

"It didn't take us long to track you down," Emma breathed. "But when we did, we realized it was too late. It had been too late for many months. Reggie was dead. Her beautiful boys didn't have a father. And to me, it looks like it's all your fault."

Grant's eyes filled with tears. Emma had never seen him lose his cool like this. Always, he'd been arrogant and sure of himself, ready with a quick joke or a witty remark.

Instead of begging for forgiveness or telling her she had it all wrong, Grant asked something that stopped Emma in her tracks.

"Are you saying I have a kid?"

Emma closed her eyes and pictured her darling baby. To her, Fiona had nothing to do with this monster before her. She shouldn't have come.

"A daughter. Fiona. She's six weeks old."

Grant's eyes pooled with tears. He sniffled and wiped them away, every bit a broken man. "Tell me what she's like. Please."

Emma dropped forward and placed her elbows on her thighs. This was a man on the brink of twenty years of prison, begging for one glimpse of what his life could have been like.

"She's so tiny, Grant. And very sweet. My mom and I have gone crazy picking out little outfits for her. She'll be spoiled rotten if we're not careful."

Grant chuckled and sniffed, somewhere in the haze of laughter and tears.

"She has blond hair and blue eyes, like my mom and I. She's got a bit of your nose. She's not smiling on purpose yet, but sometimes, an accidental smile peeks through— and I swear, it's a lot like your smile. Better, of course. But a lot like yours."

Grant hiccupped and placed his hand over his mouth, embarrassed. "Gosh. I'm sorry."

Emma laughed gently, surprised at how heartbroken she felt. "It's okay. It's a lot to take in."

Grant stared at the ground for a long time. "I know this is a lot to ask. But when I'm sent away, do you think you could send me updates on her? Like, a picture once or twice a year. Nothing major. Knowing she'll be out there, growing and changing and learning, will feel a whole lot better if I have some idea of how she's doing. Do you know what I mean?"

Emma nodded, surprised at how empathetic she felt. "I'll see what I can do."

"Thank you."

They still had a few minutes. Emma swallowed and spoke through the silence. "How did all of this happen, Grant?"

"You know, Lily asked me the same thing. It was a lot harder to answer her, though. She's my big sister. I know she expected so much more from me." He sniffed. "To be honest with you, I started thinking of life as this big game. Growing up, we never had much money. And bit by bit, I discovered ways to make it. It started small when I was a teenager. Felt so good to be able to buy my own movie tickets or take girls on dates with my own money, you know? And I had more money than most kids my age, even the kids of rich parents who were given an allowance.

"Up at Mackinac, things got out of hand. When Reggie came up to hang out with me, he was so down about Lily kicking him out of the house. He had very little money to speak of, and he'd just lost his job and was terrified to tell Lily. I told him about my connections down here in Florida, and he jumped at it. The plan was to take off, make a load of money, and then return to Michigan like kings. Reggie really did want to be there for Ralphie and Kevin. He loved those little boys like nothing else."

Emma's eyes smarted. "They're very lovable."

Grant pressed his thumbs against his eyes. His voice broke as he said, "Lily said an islander has been taking good care of her."

"Yes. My Uncle Alex."

Grant dropped his hands. "Wow. Your uncle." He considered this, his eyes far away. "Will you tell him thank you for me? Will you tell him just how much it means? I should have been there for Lily. I'll rot in that prison, thinking about all the ways I wronged her."

In a very small voice, Emma said, "I'll tell him. But know that Lily doesn't want you to rot in prison. She wants you to forgive yourself. She wants you to change." Emma shrugged and dropped her gaze. "If you can't do it for Lily, do it for your daughter."

The security guard led Emma down the hallway and into another waiting room, where Lily sat in the corner and stared at her shoes. When Emma entered, Lily leaped up and hugged Emma, shivering against her. Emma was wordless. *What was there to say?*

Back at the car, Lily turned on the radio, and they sat in the air conditioning for several minutes.

"He didn't look good," Lily breathed. "Like a shell of my little brother."

Emma nodded.

"How did he take the news about Fiona?"

"He broke down."

"I figured he would." Lily wiped away a tear. "What an idiot."

"He loves you so much," Emma reminded Lily. "He told me he'll spend the next twenty years hating himself for what he did to you."

Lily took a deep breath. Then, without answering, she shifted the gears and thrust the car from the perfect parallel parking spot and into traffic. They drove the entire way home without speaking. When they returned to the villa, Emma heard herself say, "I'm not going to the trial later."

"I wouldn't if I were you," Lily affirmed. "But I have to go. He's the only family I have left."

Chapter Twenty-One

That afternoon, Tracey, Megan, and Emma sat outside a beautiful beach restaurant and watched the waves spread themselves across the sands. A flock of seagulls squawked ahead, the V of their formation pointed south. In the distance, sailboats congregated, and around them, tanned vacationers drank oysters from shells and laughed over bottles of white wine. In every way, it was paradise. It was remarkable that miles away, Grant was being sentenced to live so much of his life behind bars.

"Did you feel anything when you saw him?" Megan asked.

Emma gazed down at her sleeping daughter in the little carrier by her chair. "I remembered things I'd once really liked about him. I remembered promises we'd made and beautiful times we'd had. But it was hard to connect those experiences with the man in front of me. He was arrested so many months ago, and he seems defeated."

"It's a tragedy," Tracey breathed.

Emma checked the time. It was thirty minutes past four, which meant that Grant's sentencing was probably already over. A few minutes later, Lily called to ask where they were. There were tears in her voice.

Emma sipped her wine and stood, stretching her arms toward the blissful sky. "I might go for a swim before Lily gets here."

"I'll watch the baby girl," Tracey said.

"Meg? You in?"

Megan nodded and leaped from her chair. Frantically, as though they were little girls again, Megan and Emma sprinted toward the waves, tearing off their beach clothes to reveal their swimsuits. Emma tried to forget the bulge of her stomach. She tried to forget the pain in her heart. As they burst into the water, Emma collapsed beneath the surface and used the breaststroke to push herself deeper into the blue. As she swam further from shore, she began to sob underwater. She forced her way back to the surface and floated for a while, grateful for the weightlessness of the ocean.

"Hey! I lost you for a second." Megan appeared beside her and treaded water.

Emma tilted her head to catch Megan's eye. "Today, I felt very old."

"You're only twenty-four, babe."

"I know that." Emma dropped her feet and treaded water, facing Megan. "But I realized how quickly our lives are going to go. By the time Grant is out of prison, Fiona will be twenty. Our moms will be in their mid-sixties. And Grandpa..." She paused, not wanting to say the unthinkable.

"It's terrifying, isn't it?" Megan grimaced.

"I think Mom should move to LA to be with Malcolm. I think everyone should experience as much life and love as possible."

Megan shook her head. "She would never leave you. You know that."

Emma's heart thudded beneath the water. Back on the

beach, Tracey had stood with baby Fiona in her arms. She peered out across the water, making sure Emma and Megan were still okay.

"You and Fiona are her life and her love. That's it. That's all she needs," Megan breathed. "In life, we have to make choices. You've made yours. Aunt Tracey has made hers."

"And you? What do you choose?"

Megan wrinkled her nose. "I'm in the process of figuring that out."

* * *

Back at the beach restaurant, Emma wrapped up in a towel and watched as Tracey placed Fiona back in her carrier. "She fell back asleep again," she explained as she poured herself a small glass of wine. "She just wanted to open her eyes for a minute to see that big, blue sky."

Suddenly, Lily stepped up to the table. She still wore her dark blue dress from the morning, and her makeup had smeared around her eyes. Megan jumped up to grab another chair as Lily tried to scold her. "Don't worry about me. I can take care of myself." Still, as Megan lined up the chair behind her, Lily collapsed into it.

Tracey ordered another bottle of wine from a passing waiter, who returned very soon after with a fresh glass. Lily thanked him and poured herself a double portion. After her first sip, she managed to say, "It's done. Twenty-five years in prison. Even more than the lawyer had guessed."

Emma's heart sank. The table was very quiet for a long time. Three tables away, a young couple uncorked a bottle of champagne, and the bubbles cascaded across their table and plates, making them laugh.

"He seemed resigned," Lily continued. "As though he'd made his peace with what he'd done. He nodded at me as they led him away, and I said quietly that I loved him. I think he understood."

"You were very brave to go," Tracey said. "I don't know if I could have done that."

"Your brother would never have done anything like this," Lily insisted. "I called Alex immediately after the sentencing. And I realized..." She closed her eyes, and a single tear escaped. "I realized he's my world now. I wouldn't know where else to turn. He's built a life for me on Mackinac, one beyond my wildest dreams."

"He loves you. I know it's been fewer than three months since you met, but that doesn't make it any less true." Tracey spoke very quietly.

"I love him, too. I told him that in the car," Lily breathed. "I think he was surprised. He said it back immediately, and then, both Ralphie and Kevin started to scream, 'I love you, Mommy!' into the phone. I burst into tears after that." Lily's voice broke. "I can't wait to go home to them. In fact, I booked a flight back to Detroit for tomorrow."

Emma understood. They all did. When you're suddenly overwhelmed with the desire to build the rest of your life with someone, a vacation in the Florida Keys is easily abandoned.

"But I hope you all enjoy the rest of your 'spring break.'" She made air quotes, which made Megan chuckle.

"We will. We'll work on our tans, have a few more nice meals, and then come back to that island of ours," Tracey said. "You can't keep us away from our home for long. It's where we belong."

* * *

The next morning, Tracey drove Lily to the airport. This left Emma, Megan, and Fiona back at the villa, where they watched the sunlight play out across the waves.

Thousands of miles away, Alex bundled up Ralphie and Kevin for the longest drive he'd taken in many years. According to Lily, the boys traveled best with sing-along songs, stuffed animals, plenty of blankets, and a seemingly endless variety of snacks. Alex followed Lily's instructions to the letter. He wanted to prove himself.

Kevin and Ralphie were very impressed with the ferry ride. Months ago, their first ride to Mackinac had been late at night, and Ralphie had been very sick, which had stunted the experience. This time, they spent the entire sixteen minutes on the top deck, screaming at the water as it rushed into violent spurts of white behind the boat. Kurt, Marcy's boyfriend, was the captain and even let Kevin and Ralphie touch the steering wheel. For hours afterward, the boys talked about the ride ecstatically. Kevin boasted he was a ship captain. Not wanting to be outdone by his older brother, Ralphie said he was, too.

Alex parked in short-term parking at the Detroit airport and hurried around the back to unlatch the kids from their car seats. He then lifted Ralphie to his chest and took Kevin's hand. As cars whizzed through the parking garage, he winced with fear that Kevin would suddenly bolt away from his hand. He'd never been more thankful for Mackinac's lack of cars. He'd never been more terrified for the boys' safety.

The airport was a chaotic blur of colors, sounds, smells, and lights. Kevin and Ralphie wanted to touch almost everything. Alex paused at a little kiosk, where he purchased hand sanitizer for about three dollars more than it should have cost. Each time Ralphie smeared his hand against a railing or a wall, Alex squirted a bit of sanitizer across his palm. How did parents do this full-time? Alex was exhausted.

When Lily had called Alex yesterday to tell him about the trial, his heart had broken for her. It now felt like eons ago that she'd arrived at the Willow Bed and Breakfast with a sick kid and another toddler, fearful and very alone. That long and winding road had led them here— and the final result was a tragedy. Still, they had each other. Lily's "I love you" had felt like sunshine on the chilliest day of the year. It had nourished Alex's soul. It had told him that, perhaps, the pain and loneliness of his past were finally finished. When she'd told him she wanted to come home immediately, he'd told her he would pick her up. He wouldn't be late.

People streamed out of the arrivals section of the airport. They were of all ages, all walks of life, and they rushed toward the loved ones who waited for them with open arms. "How was your trip?" echoed across the room. "Gosh, it's so good to see you again!" Alex held Ralphie to ensure he didn't get lost in the crowd and kept his hand latched around Kevin's.

"Where is Mommy?" Kevin asked a few times. "Is she here?"

"She'll be here," Alex affirmed. "She said she would. And your mommy doesn't lie. Remember?"

The boys nodded, sure of this more than anything else. Alex, too, was sure. He'd found a way to trust someone after years of feeling the world was out to get him.

Suddenly, Lily appeared in the crowd. She pulled her suitcase behind her, and her gorgeous brown hair streamed out in wild curls as she rushed toward them. Her smile lit up the entire room, and her eyes took in all three of them at once— Ralphie, Kevin, and Alex. Her boys. Alex felt a part of them.

"Hi! Hi!" She said it twice, then dropped down to lift Kevin up for a four-person hug. Kevin and Ralphie screeched with joy. Alex closed his eyes and kissed her as the rest of the airport guests buzzed around them. He loved this woman. He loved this life. He'd never felt more certain of anything in his life.

When the kiss broke, he echoed what everyone else had said already. "How was your trip?"

Lily smiled, grateful someone was there to ask this. "It was fine. I'm exhausted. So glad to be here."

Just like the others around him had already said, Alex echoed, "Gosh, it's so good to see you. We missed you. Didn't we, boys?"

Ralphie and Kevin nodded in agreement.

Lily blushed and kissed both of her sons on the lips. "Next time I go on vacation, I'm bringing all three of you. Deal?"

"I don't think we can argue with that," Alex said. Then, they turned together toward the exits, ready to make the long journey home.

Chapter Twenty-Two

Lily had brought her ex-husband's ashes back to Mackinac Island from Florida. For the next month, they sat in a box in the corner of the guest room Lily no longer used, as she'd moved full-time into Alex's bedroom. Alex knew better than to ask her what she wanted to do about the ashes— that she was in the midst of a private grief that he could only help her through. One morning in early May, as a gorgeous spring light fell through the curtains of their bedroom, Lily straightened her back against the bed frame, lifted her eyes to the blue sky, and said, "I want to scatter Reggie's ashes. Would you help me?"

Alex took this task very seriously. After they'd discussed the plan, he packed lunches, wine, and juice for the boys, helped Lily bundle the boys up, and guided his little blended family down to the docks, where his family boat awaited.

Because Dean had been a very passionate sailor, Alex knew the ropes well. When the boys and Lily were secure, he opened the sails so that they swelled with the wind and set them on a course toward Lake Huron. As they raced, the boys cried out with excitement. Kevin spread his arms on either side of his body, and Ralphie clapped his hands. The further they got from land, the more miraculous sailing seemed. Alex hadn't considered it in a long time, but seeing it through the little boys' eyes changed things.

Lily had decided to scatter only part of Reggie's ashes up in Mackinac. The rest she planned to give to his sister, who still lived in Detroit.

"Ralphie? Kevin?" Lily's voice was quiet as the wind whipped between them. "Do you remember what I told you about your daddy?"

Kevin and Ralphie nodded solemnly.

"You remember how he doesn't live with us on earth anymore? That he passed away?"

Again, Kevin and Ralphie nodded. As Alex stabilized the sailboat, he wondered how much the boys remembered about their father at all. Perhaps he was just a figure, an idea, like Santa Claus.

Lily adjusted the box of ashes on her lap. "In this box is a symbol of who your daddy was. It's how we remember him. And when we spread this memory through the winds over the lake, a little piece of your daddy gets to live here with us forever. Do you understand?"

Kevin furrowed his brow as Ralphie bobbed his body around. Lily had done a beautiful job of explaining, but the boys were just a little too young.

Making sure Alex had the boys secure, Lily stood, raised a handful of Reggie's ashes, and released them to the winds. Together, the four of them watched as the ashes cascaded through the air and eventually fluttered across the water.

"Wow," Kevin said, as though he was conscious of the brevity of the situation.

"Wow!" Ralphie echoed.

Lily bent back down so that her face was level with theirs.

"Remember, you can talk to your daddy any time you want to. He's in the wind and the water and the sky. Okay?"

* * *

Back at home, Alex made tea for Lily and hot chocolate for the boys. The three of them were cocooned in front of the fire, reading one of Ralphie's picture books. When Alex joined them, he sat on the couch and looked around the living room at the stacks of Legos, the stuffed animals, and the sticky crumbs on the coffee table from the boys' afternoon snack. This was what it felt like to live in a house of love. This was what safety felt like.

A few hours later, Cindy and Ron arrived to babysit the boys. Cindy carried a lasagna that she just had to pop in the oven, and Ron had brought some unique, hand-carved toys for the boys, one of a whale and another of a dolphin. Together, Cindy and Ron sat in front of the fire with Ralphie and Kevin as Lily and Alex hurried upstairs to change clothes. Ron gave the boys fact after fact about whales, which they ate up like candy.

When Lily emerged from the bathroom, Alex nearly crumbled at her beauty. She wore a sleek black dress, a pair of pearl earrings, and a puff of perfume, and her hair still held the wild curl from their sailing trip. For the thousandth time, it hit him. He was in love.

"You look gorgeous."

Lily laughed. "You clean up pretty good yourself."

"I even got the pasta sauce Kevin flung at me out of my hair," Alex pointed out.

"Very impressive." Lily dropped her gaze. She looked embarrassed yet pleased. "You've taken to this living with kids thing like a star."

Alex took her hand. With a soft yet urgent whisper, he said, "I can't think of anything else I'd rather do."

At the door, Cindy, Ron, Kevin, and Ralphie waved Alex and Lily out on their date. It had been ages since they'd gone out, just the two of them, and Lily had seen the day of spreading Reggie's ashes as the perfect opportunity.

"I just feel so much more at peace," Lily explained as they walked through the streets of Mackinac.

It was already spring, and trees and plants had begun to come alive with green buds and pink flowers. Tourists, unafraid of the evening chill, walked the streets, rode the carriages, and drank at the Pink Pony, grateful to be back on the island.

Notably, several restaurants had reopened for the spring season, which gave Alex and Lily many more choices for their date. They ended up at a steak place with an extensive wine menu, white table clothes, and a live pianist.

"In the summer, there's no way you could just walk in here," Alex explained to Lily. "They're normally booked till September."

Lily ordered the fish of the day— blue gill with roasted potatoes, while Alex opted for a juicy steak and thick-cut fries. They shared a bottle of red wine from a winery in Cadillac, Michigan, and joked about going on a winery tour later that summer if Alex could get any time off from work.

"Funny that you should mention that. I talked to my dad about hiring someone to help out with all our properties," Alex said. "It's been a ridiculous amount of work for just the two of us."

What he meant was: there was no way he would keep up that workload that summer. Not with Lily, Kevin, and Ralphie around. Dean had gotten the hint.

"We're interviewing a few candidates next week," Alex continued.

"Does that mean you're open to a wine tour?" Lily's eyes sparkled.

"I'm open to a family vacation of some kind," Alex admitted. "I don't know how much fun Ralphie and Kevin would have at a winery. But Tahquamenon Falls, for example? I think they might really get on board with that."

"I've never been there." Lily's eyes widened. "Oh gosh. The boys would love it!"

The Pink Pony was buzzing with action. Marcy held court behind the bar, stirring cocktails and chatting to tourists and locals alike as Kurt cut from table to table, trying to keep up with the orders and serving the drinks Marcy had made. A table remained empty in the corner, and Alex and Lily nabbed it. Almost as soon as they sat down, Kurt brought them a beer and a glass of wine.

"How did she know?" Lily laughed and waved to Marcy behind the counter. "Did you hear they're getting married?"

"Marcy and Kurt?" Alex let his jaw hang open. "Wow. I never in a million years thought Marcy would get married."

"Your sisters told me she almost got married a long time ago," Lily pointed out.

"Yes. It's a terrible story." Alex grimaced. He did not like thinking about poor twenty-one-year-old Marcy, left at the altar by the man she'd loved. It reminded him so much of the loneliness he'd dealt with for so many years.

"Do you believe in marriage?" Lily asked, her smile playful.

"Believe in it? Like, do I believe marriage exists?"

Lily giggled and swatted his hand. "You know that's not what I mean."

Alex sipped his beer. Was this really happening? Was the woman he was in love with asking him if he would ever consider marriage? With her?

"If I ever met the right woman, I could see myself getting married." Alex's smile was so big it hurt his face.

Lily tossed her head back with laughter. When she righted herself again, she locked eyes with him and said, "You know, that's pretty good to hear."

"Is it? Why so?"

Lily shrugged. "No reason, I guess."

Neither of them could wipe their smiles off their faces the rest of the night. To anyone else at the bar, their love was vibrant and alive, so much so that they hardly noticed anyone else in the room. *What was their secret? Why were they so happy?* Neither Lily nor Alex could have possibly answered.

Chapter Twenty-Three

Fiona was thirteen weeks old and the light of Emma's life. Strapped against Emma's chest, she cooed and wiggled, moving her little feet as Emma waited on the ferry dock, watching as Megan's ferry came closer and closer. When the dock workers heaved the ramp onto the dock, Megan was front and center, decked out in sunglasses and a baggy Michigan State sweatshirt. As soon as the ramp was secured, Megan shrieked and ran down the ramp, where she hugged Emma and kissed Fiona on the top of her head.

"She's so much bigger than she was just a few weeks ago!" Megan cried.

"Don't remind me," Emma said. "She's growing like a weed."

Megan grabbed her suitcases, which were puffy from the amount of stuff she'd pushed in them.

"We need to get a cart," Emma said. "There's no way we can wheel these up to your mom's place."

"Let's just take them to yours first," Megan said. "It's closer."

Together, Emma and Megan paused at the road, waiting as three carriages and eighteen bicyclists passed by, jangling their bells.

"Everyone's back!" Megan laughed. "Normally, it happens so gradually that I hardly notice."

"It's going to be another crazy summer," Emma agreed. She then arched her eyebrow and said, "I told you they offered us shifts at the fudge shop again this year. Right?"

Megan's jaw dropped. "You didn't!"

"Oh. Shoot. I could have sworn I texted you. Apparently, the seasonal worker they hired dropped out to follow a band around the country. They need women who know the ins and outs of the fudge business. Their words, not mine."

Megan laughed. "It really is the perfect summer job."

"Maybe we can work together for just one more year," Emma said. "This autumn, I have to get serious about what I want to become. I don't think I'll be happy if I'm forty-five and still behind the fudge counter."

Megan smiled serenely and squeezed Emma's shoulder. "Don't be too hard on yourself. You're off to a pretty good start. You're Fiona's mother. That's enough for now."

Up at Emma and Tracey's place, Tracey was in a panic. Megan and Emma found her in a heap of clothes in her bedroom, still in just her bra and underwear. Her hair curled in a million directions.

"Mom! What's up?" Emma laughed from the doorway as Megan peered over her shoulder.

Tracey turned, surprised to see them. "Megan! Welcome home!"

"Thanks, Aunt Tracey. It's good to be back." Megan tilted her head. "Are you going somewhere?"

Tracey blushed and fell back on the bed. "Girls, I don't know what to wear."

Megan and Emma stepped into the bedroom, eyeing the

long scarves, the inside-out pants, and the cream, red, and blue cardigans, all of which were strewn across the floor. It seemed Tracey had tried on just about every outfit in her closet.

"Where are you going?" Emma asked.

Tracey grimaced. She leaped to her feet and grabbed a navy-blue button-down dress, which she flung over her shoulders and began to button furiously. "It's silly, really. Terribly silly."

Emma and Megan exchanged glances. In her wrap on Emma's chest, Fiona cooed with excitement. Even she understood something was going on.

"Why would it be silly?" Emma asked.

"You're going on a date," Megan said. "This is how I act before I go out with someone I really like. It takes my apartment a week to recover."

Tracey finished buttoning her dress and twisted her body this way, then that in the mirror. "I don't know what it is."

"It's a date," Megan repeated.

Tracey turned to face them and clenched her fists at her sides. "If you must know..."

"We must know!" Emma and Megan cried at once.

"Okay." Tracey hesitated. "There are no guarantees in this life. I know that. But right now, Malcolm is flying his plane from Los Angeles to visit me. Apparently, his ex-wife has taken a job in Japan. The decision came totally out of left field."

"Japan? That's insane." Emma stepped closer to her mother. "What does that mean?"

"It goes without saying that Malcolm does not want his daughter to move to Japan," Tracey continued. "They've discussed him having full custody."

"Which would mean he could move wherever he wanted to," Emma breathed. "And bring his daughter."

Tracey frowned. "I don't want to get ahead of myself. We

haven't seen each other since Elise's wedding in October. That was seven months ago!"

"And you're even hotter than you were seven months ago, Aunt Tracey," Megan said. "How could he resist you?"

Again, Tracey dropped on the bed and placed her face in her hands. Emma and Megan sat on either side of her, Emma with her hand on Tracey's shoulder. The air around them sizzled with expectation.

"Mom! A huge film director is flying out to visit you! This is exciting!" Emma tried to pump her mother up.

Tracey shuddered. "He'll take one look at me and realize he's made a mistake."

"Why don't you give him a little more credit than that?" Emma demanded. "What you two had last summer was special. It didn't just go away. Besides. Haven't you two been talking on the phone?"

Tracey nodded. "Usually about three times a week."

Megan's jaw dropped. "From my experience with dating in East Lansing, men hate talking on the phone. If Malcolm calls you three times a week, he means business."

Little by little, Emma and Megan coaxed Tracey to the bathroom to do her makeup and hair. Within the hour, she was off to the little Mackinac Airport, where she would wait in her beautiful spring dress and watch his plane's wheels kiss the runway for the first time that year. When she disappeared around the corner, Megan and Emma screeched with excitement.

"Maybe you really can have it all," Megan said.

"What if they make movies together? Mom could be his director of costuming, and they could travel the world! We could tag along, too, of course. Me, you, and Fiona."

"Oh! I hope they film in Italy. I have dreams of dating a man from Rome." Megan laughed and returned to the kitchen, calling back, "I'm going to help myself to whatever's in your fridge. Okay?"

"You know you don't have to ask." Emma paused in the foyer for a moment, overwhelmed with a sense of happiness. The warmth of it spread to her fingers, her toes. Megan was back. Her mother might build her own happily ever after. Fiona was gorgeous and healthy. What more could she want?

* * *

Two nights later, Alex invited the family over for his first-ever all-Swartz dinner party. This was a big deal. For decades, Cindy, Tracey, and Grandpa Dean had taken the reins on such dinner parties. Alex had never felt worthy enough, as he hadn't had a family to call his own. With Lily, Kevin, and Ralphie on the island and learning, day-by-day, to build a family with Alex, it was finally time. The entire family was eager for it. If Emma had to guess, though, Alex was anxious to make everything perfect. He wouldn't be calm till it was all over.

In her bedroom, Emma dressed Fiona in an adorable pink dress with a little bow around her head, listening as Malcolm and Tracey chatted in the kitchen. Since Malcolm's arrival, the two of them had been inseparable, filling their house with near-constant laughter. Emma had texted Megan, **"They're like teenagers, I swear"**. To this, Megan had texted, **"Let Aunt Tracey have her fun!"**

When Malcolm had met Fiona, he'd asked to hold her, captivated by her little eyes and her tiny feet. "I can't believe my daughter was ever this little," he'd said. The way he'd held her, with such gentle ease, had made Emma very happy. Yes: he was a hot-shot movie director. But he was also kind, considerate, and very loyal to her mother. He passed every test.

Since Malcolm's arrival, Emma had managed to sequester her mother in the kitchen for a brief chat only once. "I think he's really going to move here, Emma. I really do. Imagine me, a stepmother to that little girl! Oh, but we're going to have to learn sign language. Are you up for that?" Emma had said she was. Then, she'd hugged her mother with tears in her eyes.

Emma carried Fiona on her chest and led Malcolm and Tracey to Alex's place a few blocks away. It was still early May, and daily temperatures rocketed to the low sixties or hung in the forties, depending on God's mood. Today, it was fifty-five and still sunny from a blissful afternoon. Behind Emma, Malcolm and Tracey chatted about the hike they'd gone on that day. As they'd walked along the lake, a fish had leaped into the sky and flapped around for a second before crashing back into the water. "It looked like he was trying to fly," Malcolm joked.

Lily opened the door to welcome them into the home she now shared with Uncle Alex. She looked serene, happy, and a little bit tan, as though she'd spent many afternoons running around with Ralphie and Kevin in the backyard or along the beach. She and Malcolm shook hands, and Lily said she was so happy to finally meet him, as she'd heard so much about him. "All good things, I hope?" Malcolm teased, side-eyeing Tracey.

Already, Cindy, Ron, Megan, Michael, Margot, and their baby, Winnie, were seated around the dining room table. Kevin and Ralphie continued to play in the living room, waiting to be called to the table. Ralphie popped up and waved to Emma and Tracey, saying, "Hi, baby Fiona." In response, Emma and Tracey said, "Hi, Ralphie! Hi, Kevin!"

Hugs were exchanged. Everyone was so happy to welcome Malcolm to Mackinac, asking him why he'd stayed away so long. Malcolm was gracious, saying all the right things as he sat next to Tracey and squeezed her hand. Emma set baby Fiona up for a nap in the next room and then grabbed a seat next to Megan, wrapping her in a hug. Alex hurried in with another few bottles of wine, his smile effervescent. Emma had never seen him happier, although he did seem jittery. "Anyone need a glass of wine?"

"Where's Dad?" Cindy asked as Alex began to pour.

"Dad, Elise, Wayne, Brad, and Penny are on their way," Alex announced. "They should be here any minute."

On cue, the doorbell rang. Lily rushed off to answer it. Soon, the sound of Grandpa Dean's booming voice filled the house. Alex hurried to greet him. Emma knew this was an important moment for him, as he wanted to prove to Grandpa Dean, once and for all, that he was a family man, just like him. Just like any child, Alex needed his father to be proud of him. It was only natural.

Elise was ecstatic to see Malcolm, whom she'd worked with on the film last summer. She hugged him and said, "Didn't I tell you Mackinac was a whole lot better than Los Angeles?"

"The traffic is certainly better," Malcolm joked. "Although I nearly got run over by a horse and buggy yesterday."

"It can happen," Grandpa Dean said gravely. "Keep your eyes peeled!"

"I will," Malcolm reported.

As Grandpa Dean sat at the head of the table, he pressed his hand over his chin and then flattened his palm forward. It was sign language for "thank you." The table quieted as they gazed at him.

"That's all I know so far," Grandpa Dean said. "But I bought an e-book that is supposed to teach you sign language this morning and plan to learn a little bit every single day. If your daughter really moves to the island with you, I'm going to want to get to know her. I hope that's okay."

Malcolm's eyes were misty. He took a sip of wine and studied Grandpa Dean, genuinely shocked.

"I'm going to learn, too," Elise announced.

"We're all going to," Cindy said. "That goes without saying."

Tracey laughed and closed her eyes, as though the love she felt was too intense.

"I can't thank you enough," Malcolm said. "I think there's more love here at this dinner table than there is across the entire state of California."

"We do what we can," Grandpa Dean said, his eyes twinkling.

Together, the Swartz Family, with the addition of the ones they loved who would one day join the Swartz Family, gathered their hands together and bent their heads in prayer. May sunlight came in heavenly rays through the large bay window. In the distance, the Straits of Mackinac glittered with promise for a brand-new era of joy.

Chapter Twenty-Four

Playtime Corner was a daycare center in downtown Mackinac Island. For years on his lunch breaks, Alex had walked past it and heard the laughter and cries of children and the caring words from the very patient women who worked there. Most were children of hospitality workers across the island. As their parents worked to create magical vacations for families from across the globe, their children tried their hardest to break the sound barrier.

Never had Alex imagined he would ever require Playtime Corner's services. But now, things had changed. It was late May, which meant tourism season had ramped up considerably. Although Dean and Alex had hired someone to take on some of Alex's responsibilities for the bed and breakfasts and hotels across the island, they still needed a little bit of help. Lily had asked if she could join them to tie up loose ends, work front desks, or do a little secretary work here and there. This was beyond Alex's wildest dreams. In the old days, Alex's mother and father had worked side-by-side, ensuring the many Swartz properties were taken care of. Now, Lily and Alex would do the same. Together.

Now, Lily and Alex stood in the foyer of Playtime Corner and chatted with the head caretaker, a woman in her thirties in a bright pink shirt. She had glitter on her face from a crafting accident, and she seemed to speak perpetually in song.

"We welcome Kevin and Ralphie to Playtime Corner!" She squatted to give the boys high-fives. "Are you ready to have fun?"

Kevin and Ralphie raced off to join the other kids, who showed them where the crayons and coloring books were located. Lily watched them and chuckled. "It'll be hard to get them to leave later today."

"We find the children wear themselves out here and are very ready to be taken home by five o'clock," the woman who worked there said. "Remember. Five o'clock pick-up." For a moment, her face changed. "It's important our parents are not late."

Alex and Lily assured her they wouldn't be. Alex was incredibly happy to hear himself referred to as a "parent." He wasn't sure he would ever get over it.

Back outside, Lily cackled and said, "That woman is a saint. It's hard enough watching two little boys, let alone fifteen to twenty little kids who want to throw glitter on you all day."

"She has a few other people helping her," Alex pointed out.

Lily gave him a stern look. "They're all saints."

"You're right." Alex joined her laughter and laced his hand around her waist. Together, they walked toward the main Swartz office, where they planned to outline the week's responsibilities and separate tasks.

On the way to the office, they stumbled into Elise and Penny, who were out for a jog. Penny gasped for breath dramatically and said, "I can't believe people do this for fun." She loosened her long blonde hair from an elastic and smiled at Lily. Everyone always smiled at Lily. Alex's chest filled with pride just to be in her midst.

"Where are you two off to?" Elise asked.

"We're going to work," Lily said. "I've been officially hired by the Swartz Estate." She squeezed Alex's hand.

"That's incredible!" Elise cried. "Alex, you always worked way too hard. I hope Lily can reel you in a little bit this summer, so you can have some actual fun."

"Don't worry. My main mission this summer is fun," Lily told her conspiratorially.

"Ours, too." Penny laughed. "You should see the list of activities we have planned. We put the list on the fridge. Wayne is already overwhelmed."

"So, you're staying on Mackinac all summer long again?" Alex asked.

"Yes. Brad talked me into it," Penny said. "I just finished shooting the pilot of a TV show, and we're waiting to hear if it'll become a series or not. Fingers crossed!"

"You deserve it, Penny. From what I've heard from your mom, you've worked so hard to get where you are," Lily said.

Penny and Elise continued their run, heading east toward the Island House to eventually loop around Arch Rock. Along the docks, around fifty sailboats were tied, shifting in the light spring breeze. Alex inhaled the intoxicating smell of lilac bushes, which had already begun to bloom across the island in preparation for the upcoming Lilac Festival. Just like last year, Cindy and Ron had joined forces and planned to have an even more action-packed schedule. As Alex and Lily walked the rest of the way to the Swartz office, Alex explained the importance of the Lilac Festival, that early settlers of Mackinac Island had brought the first lilac bushes from Europe. When Alex finished his monologue, Lily paused at the corner near the fudge shop and tugged Alex back into her, kissing him gently as a horse and buggy clopped past.

"What was that for?" Alex asked.

"I just love when you get all nerdy about history." Lily pressed her nose against his.

Alex blushed violently. "Is it really that nerdy?"

"If you ask me, the world needs a few more nerds like you."

On the second story of a downtown building sat the Swartz Family office. Once there, Alex and Lily divided their tasks, and Lily donned a pair of reading glasses that made her look adorable. For hours, she bent toward the office computer and read contracts and spreadsheets with incredible ease. Twice, she paused to ask Alex a question, which he was happy to answer. By lunchtime, they'd completed more tasks than Alex could have possibly gotten through on his own.

When they paused to head to The Grind for some food, Lily received a text message from Emma. "Apparently, one of Emma's friends here on the island is pregnant. She's looking for a midwife." Lily smiled and placed her phone in her pocket, then whipped her spring jacket around her shoulders.

"Wow! What do you think of that?"

"I love being a midwife. I really do. But I'm not sure if I can take the job on."

"If you'd rather work as a midwife than work here at the Swartz office, I understand," Alex said, suddenly worried he was distracting Lily from what she really wanted to do. He opened the door for Lily, who stepped forward and walked down the staircase toward the vibrant street below.

"It's not that," Lily said. "It's really fun to work with you."

"It's only been one day. Maybe by the end of summer, I'll drive you crazy."

"I don't think that's possible." Lily kept smiling and slid her hand through his as they walked toward The Grind. In front of them, a little girl ate an ice cream cone, and her chin was coated with chocolate.

"But I'm sure you'd have time to work as a midwife and work here at the office with me," Alex said. "We can be flexible about it."

"It just doesn't make sense."

"Why not?" Alex pushed it, sensing there was something he was missing.

Lily paused, watching as a horse and buggy clopped by. Very quietly, she said, "By the time this young woman gives birth, I'll already be seven months pregnant. If I remember the third trimester correctly, I'll be too exhausted to be a midwife. I'll be too exhausted to do anything but eat pizza and hang out."

Alex's jaw dropped. For a full ten seconds, only the sound of his heartbeat filled his ears. Had he heard her correctly? Was he going crazy?

"Lily. What are you saying?"

Lily turned, and her eyes sparkled. "You know what I'm saying."

Alex stuttered. "You're...pregnant?"

"I am."

Around Alex, the world seemed to stop spinning. All he knew was this woman before him, the woman who'd changed his life forever when she'd stumbled into the Willow with a million secrets and two little boys.

Lily placed her hand on Alex's cheek. They held each other's gaze for a long time.

"I love you, Lily," Alex said. His eyes filled with tears.

"I love you, too. And this baby loves you. We can't wait to live the rest of our lives with you if you'll have us."

Coming Next by Katie Winters

You can now Pre Order Nantucket in Bloom

Other Books by Katie

Connect with Katie Winters

BookBub
Facebook
Newsletter

To receive exclusive updates from Katie Winters please sign up
to be on her Newsletter!
CLICK HERE TO SUBSCRIBE

Made in the USA
Monee, IL
02 March 2023

29035668R00098